A Small Piece of Her Heart

By Corine Marie

To every reader, may you experience divine love.

A Small Piece of Her Heart

Chapter One

AUBREY SPRINTS down the track, her arms pumping and her knees lifting powerfully. She is the first to cross the finish line. Her opponents cross a second later, huffing and gasping for air. Aubrey stands statuesque, calm, and composed as if she can go another round.

Stepping onto the winner's podium, Aubrey takes the number one spot and receives her gold medal. Her teammate, Jade, stands in the second-place position, glaring enviously at Aubrey from the corner of her eye. Aubrey turns toward Jade and smiles. Sucking her teeth, Jade steps off the podium. Aubrey looks at her other teammate and best friend, Lily. The two of them snicker among themselves.

"That girl thinks the sun comes up just to hear her crow," Lily states.

Aubrey giggles at how Lily emulates her southern grandma, void of the accent.

The crowd disperses from the stands as Aubrey frees her feet from her track spikes. A group of children bounce excitedly, waiting for Aubrey to walk by. They wave when she reaches them. Aubrey waves back, flashing a smile, and their little faces gleam. Unfortunately, Aubrey doesn't notice her moment of fame. Lily, straining her neck, and looking through the crowd, consumes Aubrey. "There's my mom," Lily announces. "Be right back."

Lily runs into her mom's arms. A sincere smile covers Aubrey's face at the sight of Lily and her mother hugging. They look more like sisters with matching long black hair and striking green eyes. Watching them gives her a warm feeling but also pricks her heart. She looks away only for her gaze to land on Jade, laughing with her parents. In fact, most athletes are having a moment with their parents. Aubrey's eyes drop. She feels a burn in her nose traveling up to sting her eyes. Puddles begin forming, obstructing her view. She refuses to allow the tears to fall. Removing the gold medal from her neck, she spreads her legs wide and bends forward, stretching her hamstrings. Maintaining movement keeps the desolation from creeping in.

Across the track, Coach Aaron speaks with an athlete who transferred from the University of Texas. "I'm ecstatic to have you; you're an amazing athlete. However, we do things differently here." Coach Aaron points proudly at the CSU logo on his t-shirt, an abbreviation for Centered State University. "This isn't your typical college. We have mentors instead of professors because we care about the person you're becoming more than the money you'll make. Your salary is secondary to your character. We won't tolerate any trouble."

He doesn't respond to Coach Aaron. Instead, his attention is on Aubrey across the track. She had first captured his focus during the track meet. Aubrey ran her races with authority and power. He couldn't focus on anyone other than her. She moves with such easy strength that both intrigues and attracts him. The attraction feels foreign to him, much different than his attraction to previous women. Her physical isn't what's making him rise, though she is stunning. It is her energy. He can feel her emanating electrically despite the thousands of square feet between them. Looking away from her isn't a choice for him. He watches her, binging her world. He observes her sitting alone while everyone else revels in family adoration. Where is her fan section, he wonders. She deserves love and praise like the other runners. He wants to give her what he feels she is due.

"Did you hear what I said?" Coach Aaron deepens his tone.

"Yes sir," he answers swiftly, snapping out of his trance. "I guarantee you won't have any trouble with me."

"Good." Coach Aaron puts his whistle in his mouth, giving it two gentle blows. "Everybody gather around. I want to introduce our newest teammate."

As Aubrey walks over, she makes eye contact with the new teammate. They lock gazes, two pairs of matching brown eyes allured by an indescribable force. Typically, she wouldn't flatter any male by staring, but his presence demands her attention. She wills herself to look away, but his eyes won't release hers. For moments, she is his prisoner, unsure she wants an escape. Then, he drops his gaze, releasing her, which annoys Aubrey. She isn't annoyed because she wants more of his attention but because she has already given too much of herself by relinquishing more than a glance.

"Everybody, this is Daniel Sane," Coach introduces. "Let's welcome him to the sprint squad."

Lily leans over to whisper in Aubrey's ear. "You know who he is, right?"

Aubrey recognizes his name. Every sports station mentioned Daniel Sane daily. He is a football luminary—most likely a first-round NFL draft pick. Aubrey frowns, curious why he is joining the track team in Ohio. Acknowledging Lily's question, she nods. "Wonder what he's doing here?"

The team surrounds Daniel, welcoming him. The women—particularly Jade—shower him with attention. Deciding not to participate, Aubrey waves at Daniel halfheartedly before walking away. The corners of Daniel's mouth lift into a small smile, half offended and half amused.

Once the crowd clears, the team captain approaches Daniel. "Hey, bro. My name is Travis, but everyone calls me Trav."

As Travis is introducing himself, students passing by interrupt them. A few girls wave and Travis responds with a cool nod. One guy acknowledges him with a quick handshake. A second guy stops to talk. "Trav! Last week's pool party was on point. When's the next event?"

"I'll let you know," Travis says before returning his attention to Daniel.

"Seems like you're the man around here," Daniel recognizes.

"Eh, I do what I can to bring the people together. I know all the ins and outs on campus, so if you need anything—"

"Who is she?" Daniel asks immediately. He looks directly at Aubrey, but Travis doesn't see past Jade.

A naughty smirk settles on Trav's face. "That's Jade. You'll like her."

Daniel wags his head impatiently. "Not Jade." He nods in Aubrey's direction. "Her." They watch Aubrey gather her natural curls into a bun. She slides a jacket over her sports bra, flips the hood, and hides her eyes with sunglasses.

"Nah, bro." Travis enunciates his words intricately while wildly shaking his head. "Too much work! Stick with Jade."

Daniel laughs at his dramatic display. "Appreciate the info." Daniel's gaze remains on Aubrey, further intrigued. He isn't the type to shy away from women who are considered too much. He will always choose abundance when choosing between plenty or a lack of a woman.

Aubrey puts on her backpack and takes out her car keys.

"You aren't coming out to eat with us?" Lily asks theatrically as if Aubrey is insulting her.

"You know you're more than welcome, honey," Lily's mom adds.

Aubrey would accept the invitation to hang out with the mother-daughter duo any other day, allowing their identical personalities to entertain her. But the two of them evoke unwelcome thoughts of her mom. "Thanks, Mrs. Landers. I'm not hungry. I'll catch up with you ladies another day." Aubrey waves and leaves the indoor arena.

She cruises with her windows down, watching the students on campus. There is a diverse crowd of joyful people in front of the dorms. Outside of Power Hall, they eat dinner picnic-style. At Light Residence, the students sit in a large circle, playing a rowdy game. Their laughter is boisterous, causing Aubrey to laugh along with them. In front of Culture Hall, one of the CSU's mentors teach while the students hang on to her every word. After ten minutes of driving, Aubrey pulls in front of Truth Residence Hall and parks in the student lot. She gathers her things before stepping out of her corroding Honda. She waves at the students lounging in the grass area as she enters the building.

The moment she walks inside, a pristine Audi pulls into the parking lot, taking the open space next to her car. Daniel Sane hops out of the car and starts crossing the parking lot. He scrolls through his phone as he walks, only looking up to check for vehicles. When Daniel enters the building, his phone continues to occupy his attention. It's not until he looks up to check his surroundings that he notices Aubrey Blake in the lobby. She stands in front of the elevator, waiting for it to arrive. Daniel slides his phone into his pocket. He approaches Aubrey, needing to see her eyes again. When she had looked at him earlier, she seemed so familiar. Racking his brain, he tries to remember if he has met her. Perhaps he recognized her from television or social media? Instinctively, he knows it's neither because she isn't the type of woman he would forget. Needing to see her eyes up close, he stares, waiting for her to cooperate.

Feeling a presence, Aubrey turns her head. The glance turns into a doubletake when she recognizes his flawless melanin skin, perfect smile, and profound eyes. Aubrey shifts her sunglasses to the top of her head, daring to examine him so closely. Just as he had captured her before, Daniel takes her away again, away from whatever world exists around them. The force between them transports them somewhere beyond logic. They both innately know that they have a purpose together, and life is shifting them, tapping them on the shoulder, beckoning them to be receptive.

Daniel extends his hand to her. "Hi, my name is Daniel Sane." The words glide out his mouth in a deep, gentle, serene sound. The depth in his voice matches his tall and muscular frame. The gentle tone harmonizes with his soft eyes.

She hesitates to connect with his open hand, fearful because there is too much power between them. It will be simple for him to penetrate her with just a touch. Aubrey delicately places her hand in his. His skin feels warm against her skin. The heat emitting from his body makes her shudder instead of bringing her warmth. Aubrey pulls her hand away quickly. Daniel keeps his hand open, feeling her touch linger. He wants more, but he knows it is all she will give. Daniel sees that she feels the same tapping on the shoulder as he does. Life is beckoning her too, but she's going to fight it. Doesn't she know her arms are too short to throw hands with divine powers?

"I know who you are," Aubrey responds softly. "We met already." She is somewhat offended that he forgot her so quickly.

Daniel flashes a smile that sends Aubrey's heartbeat on a wild ride. Something about it reminds her of childhood. Maybe it's the innocence in his eyes or the joy within. "Actually, you're the only one of my teammates who didn't speak to me."

"I said hi to you," Aubrey defends.

"You waved."

"Exactly. I said hi," she reiterates.

His smile grows into a grin. He is enjoying himself. Aubrey can't deny that she also enjoys the moment, though she keeps her face composed. She doesn't want to smile at the man and give him the impression that he can just walk through the walls she built up and renovate the place. But then, she wonders what color he would paint the walls.

"What are you doing here?" she asks as the elevator doors open.

"I live here," he replies, walking into the elevator. He reaches his arm through the opening as if holding the door for her.

Aubrey slowly steps into the elevator, her head spinning. She watches Daniel push the third-floor button. Her mouth drops open. "You moved into the apartment on the third floor?"

Daniel nods gently.

Aubrey takes a moment to swallow back the shock. "We're neighbors," she says in a shaky voice.

Chapter Two

AUBREY AND DANIEL stand quietly as the elevator doors close. Aubrey seems like she prefers to be anywhere else but in the confined space with him. She twiddles with one of the straps on her backpack restlessly. Daniel mashes his thick lips together to avoid erupting into laughter. "Don't look so distressed," he teases. "I won't ask to borrow any brown sugar or anything." The corners of Aubrey's mouth twitch as she fights a smile, and Daniel is proud of himself for loosening her up. "You ran great today," he compliments, keeping the conversation alive. "I honestly enjoyed watching you."

"Thank you."

"Your parents must live too far away to be at every meet?" he asks casually. Aubrey's twiddling ceases, and her entire body goes stiff. She observes him as he observes her— Daniel awaiting an answer, Aubrey thinking of something to say but coming up with nothing. Finally, after a moment of painful silence, Daniel realizes he has said something wrong. He just doesn't know what. "I mean, uh … I just noticed that they weren't there," he adds, fumbling over his words. "If I enjoyed you, I could only imagine how proud of you they are."

The elevator doors open, and Aubrey walks out without an answer to his question. She doesn't know how to explain her wounds to the familiar stranger. Aubrey walks across the hall to her apartment door. She shoves the key into the lock and turns the knob. She doesn't walk in. It doesn't feel right to walk away, leaving words unsaid. Looking back at Daniel, Aubrey forces a pleasant expression on her face. "See you around, teammate … neighbor," she says, ending the conversation correctly.

"Have a goodnight, Aubrey," Daniel utters quietly, feeling bad about whatever happened.

Stepping inside her apartment, Aubrey exhales a sigh of relief, glad to be free from his question and mesmerizing presence. She drops her keys on a plastic bin that doubles as her clothing drawer and a makeshift end table. She places her backpack next to a basic futon—the only piece of furniture in her apartment—and goes into the kitchenette. Aubrey opens the cabinet and removes the single dish inside—a clear glass bowl. Next, she opens the drawer and retrieves the only spoon inside. Taking a step back, she crosses her arms, carefully contemplating her dinner options, five boxes of cereal lined up on the counter. The Peanut Butter Crunch wins. She fills her bowl, lights a candle, and savors every bite while enjoying her company.

NEXT DOOR, Daniel drizzles olive oil in a stainless-steel pan before adding an array of chopped vegetables. He expertly sprinkles pink salt, garlic powder, and lemon pepper over the vegetables, carefully covering every inch while dabbing his fingers on a white towel over his shoulder. He opens the oven, studying the chicken filets cooking inside.

"Knock, knock," a voice breaks his focus. He looks up from the oven to see his sister kicking off her stilettos and closing the door behind her. "It's smelling good in here."

"Kennedy," Daniel announces her name playfully, dragging out the end. "What up, sis?"

"I brought you something." She sits her designer purse on Daniel's black leather sofa and takes out a sterling silver photo frame. She carefully lowers it to the glass end table, positioning it until it is correct. "It's the picture Mom sent us this morning from Hawaii." Removing the towel from his shoulder, Daniel wipes his hands and tosses the towel on the counter. He walks over to stand next to Kennedy. They stare blankly at the photo. "Doesn't she look happy? I put up the same picture in my place," Kennedy tells him.

In a sudden movement, Daniel reaches out and turns the frame face down.

"Daniel!" Kennedy shrieks.

"Come on, let's eat," he says, walking away as if nothing happened.

Kennedy lets out a sympathetic sigh before following her brother into the kitchenette.

Meanwhile, next door, Aubrey showers and squeezes into her favorite cutoff shorts made from her middle-school sweatpants. She pairs the cutoffs with a sports bra and plops down on her futon, bringing her knees to her chest. She touches her phone screen to check the time. It is 7:37 in the evening. She breathes a small sigh, desolately glancing around at the empty walls of her apartment. Releasing another sigh, she opens the plastic bin and takes out a journal. She searches through the pages until she finds the page she is looking for. Across the top of the page are the words *Ways to Calm & Regroup*, followed by a numbered list. Number one on the list instructs her to be still. The second point leads her to breathe deeply. Aubrey closes her eyes. She sucks in a breath and releases it. Aubrey inhales another breath, sucking in her stomach simultaneously until it can't pull in any further. Slowly and softly, the air seeps from her lips. She continues deep breathing until she enters rest.

THE NEXT MORNING, Aubrey wakes up at four o'clock. She brews her favorite lemon tea and sips from an aesthetically pleasing clear mug. She cracks the blinds, welcoming in the city's street lights until the sun replaces them. She lights a lavender candle, unrolls a stretching mat, and begins her morning routine. She sits still and breathes deeply, sipping tea occasionally. When she finishes meditating, she stands, reaching her arms above her body. She strains until she can't stretch herself any further. She bends over to touch her toes and lifts herself into a handstand. She hangs out upside-down momentarily before letting her body slump onto the mat. Finally, she is ready to begin her day.

Aubrey dresses in her usual—a sports bra and leggings. She grabs a granola bar and heads out the door. She walks into the hallway. Daniel is standing by the elevator. Her heartbeat increases instantly. How could she have forgotten he lived next door?

"Good morning," he greets, his deep voice pleasantly soothing.

"Morning. On your way to the weight room?" she asks, already knowing the answer. Six a.m. weight training is mandatory. He is on the team, so of course, that's where he is going.

"Yep. You?" Daniel asks just for conversation.

"Mm hmm," she confirms.

The elevator doors open, and they walk in. Aubrey places herself in a corner, folds her arms, and turns her body away from him. She scrolls through her phone, looking at nothing. Daniel takes the opposite corner, giving her the space she appears to seek. While she isn't looking, he studies her. She is like art to him—mysterious, compelling, and stunning. She seems delicate yet strong and confident. It isn't the kind of confidence that comes from trust and reliance. It is a confidence that derives from surviving and experiencing that she couldn't be broken. As he studies her, he finds himself becoming extremely inquisitive. He wants to know everything about her. The elevator opens, and they exit side by side through the lobby.

"Since we're both going to the same place and leaving practice tonight at the same time, we might as well ride to campus together," Daniel suggests with a smile.

They walk outside the building and stand in the parking lot. "I don't really know you like that," she says kindly, hoping not to offend him. "So, I'm going to drive myself." Something about him feels safe and comfortable, but she is self-protective, so she rejects the feeling and his offer.

Daniel and Aubrey get into their cars. They pull away from Truth Residence Hall one after the other. As Aubrey drives, she keeps checking her rearview mirror, seeing Daniel's car behind her. She can't help but smile at how ridiculous it is to take two vehicles to the same place. When they finally reach the arena, Aubrey pulls into a parking spot outside the weight room. Daniel pulls into the spot next to her. She steps out of her car. He steps out of his. They close their doors simultaneously and begin walking toward the entrance. "How was your drive," Daniel asks with a smirk. Aubrey laughs. Daniel laughs too. They are still laughing when they walk through the door together, causing everyone on the team to stop what they are doing to stare at them. Aubrey recognizes that everyone is questioning their togetherness. Hating to be the center of attention, she quickly pivots away from him.

"Good morning, everyone," Coach welcomes. "Today, we're doing dumbbell burnouts." Pure delight is on Coach's face as he announces the strenuous workout. "This won't be easy, so partner up and support each other." Coach points to Daniel. "Since you're working on getting back in shape, I want you to partner with Aubrey. She'll push you."

Aubrey picks up a twenty-pound dumbbell while everyone else grabs a ten-pound. She sits the dumbbell in front of Daniel. "You're an elite athlete. You can handle it," she encourages, reading the apprehension on his face. "I'll go first." Aubrey gets in position and looks toward Coach, waiting for him to start the time.

"First group, you're up. We're starting with sumo squats. Remember, it's burnouts, so go until you physically can't do anymore."

Coach blows his whistle, and the first group begins their sumo squats. Daniel tries not to gawk at Aubrey but can't look away. She squats with strength and poise superior to her teammates. It's like she is dancing while everyone else struggles to stay on their feet. After fifty reps, everyone except Aubrey has burned out. With closed eyes, she holds onto her dumbbell moving up and down effortlessly. She has mastered how to block out the burn.

"How many is that?" Coach asks.

She lowers down to complete one more squat. "One hundred."

"Alright, that's enough. Good job."

She hands the dumbbell to Daniel. He reluctantly takes hold of it, knowing he will fall short of one hundred reps. "It's been a while since I last worked out," he delivers the disclaimer.

"Well, you're already doing amazing simply because you are back out here, so great job," Aubrey says. Coach blows his whistle, and the second group begins. After thirty reps, Daniel starts to move a bit slower. "You got it," Aubrey cheers for him.

Not wanting to look weak in front of her, he pushes through the pain. Once he gets to his fiftieth rep, his legs shake. He is grunting. His body wants to give up, but Daniel doesn't want to be the first in the second group to burn out.

"You're done, Sane," Coach calls out.

Daniel doesn't stop. His body trembles as he lowers down into another squat. Coach blows his whistle. "Stressing out your muscles will do more harm than good. Just trust the process, and you'll catch up."

Daniel drops his weights and head, embarrassed he did fewer reps than Aubrey. He is supposed to be a superior athlete with aspirations to play professionally. As he beats himself up, he peeks to see if his teammates are judging him. The only person looking in his direction is Aubrey. She lifts her chin, wanting him to follow suit. Daniel mimics her, lifting his chin.

"When I first did burnouts, I only got to seventeen," she tells him with the most reassuring smile. Daniel's whole world stops as he takes a moment to appreciate her intentional encouragement. She doesn't know what he has been through, yet she uplifts him. He permits himself to bask in her presence, wondering who this woman is and why she seems so enthralling.

"Grab a drink," Coach instructs.

Aubrey prances away as if she hasn't done one hundred squats while Daniel struggles to lift his legs. Travis grabs Daniel's water bottle and meets Daniel halfway. "You alright, bro?" Travis examines him.

"I'm good! Aubrey is goals!"

"Because she doesn't have anything better to do other than workout. She doesn't have a life," Travis interjects harshly. Daniel ignores his negativity toward Aubrey. In his experience, the only time a male spoke badly about a female was when he couldn't have his way with her. "If you want to meet some girls, come to my cookout this weekend," Travis invites.

The only girl Daniel wants to get to know is Aubrey. "Did you invite Aubrey and Lily?" he questions.

Travis looks at Daniel, wondering why he isn't heeding his warning. "She's not going to come. Lily will, but Aubrey won't."

"Invite her anyway," Daniel suggests.

Travis doesn't want to invite her. He does not want her unpleasant energy at his cookout. Travis turns away from Daniel, unwilling to budge on his decision.

Daniel lets out a huff. "I'm trying to see something," Daniel explains. "You invite her. I let her know that I plan to be there, and if she shows up, she came to see me."

Travis throws up his hands, conceding. "Alright."

Across the track, Aubrey settles next to Lily, gulping her water. "I noticed how Daniel Sane watched you squat," Lily confronts. "And I didn't miss you two walking in here together."

Aubrey rolls her eyes. "Don't start."

"Tell me what's going on?" Lily is confident that there is something to tell.

"Nothing." She avoids eye contact with Lily.

"I've been knowing you since cat was a kitten. So I know when something's up," Lily challenges.

"Clearly, you don't."

"Okay…" Lily puts her hands on the ground, preparing to push herself to her feet and walk over to Daniel. Instead, Aubrey grabs her arm, pulling her back. Lily isn't the type to bluff. She is about her business and Aubrey's business too.

"Why are you like this?" Aubrey asks with a smile.

Lily huffs out a sigh. "Now, you're stalling."

Aubrey shrugs one shoulder, feigning indifference. "He's my neighbor," she says, telling Lily what she wants to hear.

Lily's green eyes grow wide as her head fills with ideas. "So, you've had time with him alone?"

"Briefly. He congratulated me on my win yesterday and said he enjoyed watching me run."

"He was flirting with you. Did you flirt back?" Lily leans in. She is bouncing in anticipation.

"You just said you knew me, right?"

Lily's shoulders fall into a slumped position as she groans loudly. Indeed, she knows her best friend. Aubrey isn't going to flirt with anyone, anywhere, ever. "Why are *you* like this?"

Lily is in the middle of a dramatic meltdown when Travis approaches. "What's up, ladies?" Travis greets in his usual cocky manner. "I'm having a cookout this weekend, and you're both invited."

Travis' entire existence rubs Aubrey the wrong way. She hates how he constantly treats women like it is their pleasure to be around him. Aubrey opens her mouth to decline the invitation, but Lily is quicker.

"We'll be there!"

"Cool," Travis replies simply before walking away.

Aubrey shoots her a questionable look. "Since when do we hang out with Travis?"

"Since Travis started hanging with Daniel."

"I'm not going."

"Can you remove the out-of-order sign from your heart for five minutes to see where this goes?" Lily begs.

Aubrey glowers. "Don't use your therapist jargon with me."

"Mindset Expert," Lily corrects.

"Mindset Expert," Aubrey repeats dubiously. "Is that a psychology degree alternative?"

"A degree is so 2001. It doesn't take six years of school to see that you isolate yourself to avoid pain, thus never experiencing life."

Aubrey ignores her, turning to watch Travis approach Daniel. He whispers to Daniel, causing Daniel to look in Aubrey's direction. They maintain eye contact. It is comfortable. Aubrey looks away when she feels like he is invading her world.

Chapter Three

AFTER THE MORNING WORKOUT, Daniel wrestles to get Aubrey out of his thoughts. He keeps thinking of her throughout his classes. Her ambiguous demeanor frustrates him. He wants to know what she feels when she looks at him. Later that evening, during track practice, Daniel tries to catch her gaze again. Every chance he gets, he puts himself in her line of sight, but Aubrey won't look at him. She purposely avoids making eye contact. Perhaps she doesn't feel the same pulsing in her veins he feels when she is near. Daniel is okay with that possible truth. There is so much going on in his life that he doesn't have time to entertain a woman anyhow. The number one goal on his hefty to-do list is getting back in shape. Ironically, he is in the middle of a workout, trying to get a woman's attention. Using his inward voice, he gives himself a pep talk, reminding himself of his goals. After the pep talk, he powers through the workout.

Practice ends, and Daniel catches Aubrey scurrying out the door. To evaluate his attraction to her, he waits about five minutes before heading to his car. Sure, she is beautiful, but there are beautiful women everywhere. Why her? And why now, at such a crucial time in his life?

Daniel saunters to his car. As he approaches, he sees Aubrey fumbling through her bags. The moment Daniel walks up, she seemingly discovers her keys. Her ploy to wait for him is obvious. Daniel's resolve to keep his distance fades. He leans against his car, smiling at her. She opens her back door and puts away her bags. She peeks up, giving him her eyes. Daniel dances inside.

"What?" she asks innocently as if she didn't wait for him. Daniel recognizes her game, and he is eager to play.

"I saw you looking at me earlier." He says the first thing that comes to his mind.

"I was looking at Travis standing next to you."

Daniel barks out a laugh. "Okay." He hardly knows Travis and Aubrey, but it isn't hard to miss that they aren't harmonious with each other. Aubrey also giggles, unable to keep a straight face. Her nose wrinkles and her eyes sparkle. In that quick moment, watching her laugh, Daniel notices a different side of her. There is a soft, lightheartedness he finds adorable. "Are you going to Trav's cookout?" he asks, needing to know when he will get more time with her.

Aubrey's almond-shaped eyes narrow as she thinks about it. She wants to remove the out-of-order sign, at least temporarily, since she doesn't immediately say no as she did to Lily. However, she isn't too hasty. She decides to take her time and think about it. "Possibly," she responds with a small smile.

Daniel predicts, from how she smiles at him, that *possibly* means yes.

THE AUGUST HEAT isn't what causes Daniel to sweat. The wait for Aubrey has him flustered. He listens impatiently as Travis babbles while manning the grill. Daniel searches for Aubrey's face every five minutes to see if she snuck in without him noticing. He gets irritated each time he looks up, and she is not there.

"I told you she wasn't going to come," Travis comments casually, setting out a platter of overcooked chicken to serve to his guests.

Just as Travis makes the statement, Aubrey walks into his backyard. Daniel sits up straight, his mood instantly shifting. Whatever Travis says no longer matters; Daniel's entire attention belongs to Aubrey. Despite her lack of trying, she is easily the most beautiful woman at the cookout. She wears a similar outfit daily—a sports bra and matching leggings, while the other women dress to impress.

"Aubrey is far from basic," Travis admits, "but she's a heartbreaker. I'm trying to warn you, bro."

Daniel whips his head in Trav's direction, interested in what he has to say.

"What do you mean?"

"All I know—" Travis begins his gossip, waving his spatula around as he talks. "She was dating some dude last year. He would show up at practices looking for her. She would hide in Coach's office while dude begged to talk to her. Apparently, she ghosted him— changed her number and moved to a different place without letting him know why. So Coach had to ban him from showing up. I felt bad for the dude. She didn't have to do him like that."

Daniel turns away from Travis and back to Aubrey, pondering the intel. None of it changes his mind; it only makes him more interested in her. As Daniel is about to fulfill his sole purpose for being at the cookout, a group of women sashay in front of him. Jade is leading. She twirls one of her big golden curls that matches her unblemished golden skin, attempting to tantalize Daniel.

"Hey, superstar," she sings in a delicate voice.

"Hey. It's Jane, right?" Daniel asks, hoping it is her name. He recalls her beauty and her desperation but forgets her name.

"Jade with a D," she corrects. His mishap doesn't offend her. "If you're free later, I'd like to give you a campus tour. Show you the stuff the guides don't know about."

Across the yard, Aubrey and Lily take selfies. After snapping each photo, Lily looks over her shoulder at the girls surrounding Travis and Daniel. "Enough photos," Lily says, standing. "Let's go."

Aubrey deciphers Lily's mischief. She can see it in her eyes. "Go where?" Aubrey questions.

"To make our presence known," Lily answers as if it's obvious.

"We're fifty feet away. Our presence is known. Men are going to do what they're going to do. So it's better to sit back and let them reveal themselves."

Lily crosses her arms and pops her hip. "I'm going. Are you coming or not?"

Aubrey looks at Lily from the side of her eye. "Is this about Daniel or Travis?" she interrogates.

"Travis," Lily replies bluntly. "I'm not afraid to say I like somebody."

Aubrey rolls her eyes and points to Lily's seat. "We're going to sit down and give them a chance to walk over and approach us."

Lily looks over her shoulder again at the girls flirting with Travis and Daniel. She feels like she needs to disrupt and take control. "I'm going," she tells Aubrey.

"I'm not coming." Aubrey remains solid in her stance.

Lily walks away, leaving Aubrey sitting alone at the fold-out table. Aubrey takes out her phone and starts scrolling. Several minutes pass before she feels a presence take the seat next to her. His smell hits her first. The scent is intoxicatingly pleasant. Looking out the corner of her eye, she recognizes Daniel's flawless dark skin and bright smile.

"I brought you some food." He puts a plate in front of her. Aubrey looks at the burger, kebab, and dry chicken breast, trying not to cringe. "It wasn't many options," Daniel continues.

"Thank you." Aubrey picks up the kebab just to be friendly and starts nibbling. Daniel picks up the burger, taking it out of the wrapper. "Don't eat that," Aubrey warns.

Daniel looks at the burger with a perplexed expression.

"Those are from a place called Sloppy Burger. They're only ninety-five cents. You will be on the toilet for days."

Daniel drops the burger back onto the plate, and they laugh. "What took you so long to get here?" Daniel asks candidly.

Aubrey stops chewing to ponder the true meaning of his question. Is he directly telling her that he had been waiting for her? A tingling starts in her stomach, quickly spreading to reach her fingers and toes. The feeling is warming and new. She likes it. "I was deciding if I wanted to come or not. I'm not the socialite type."

"So, what made you come? Was it me?"

The answer to his question is yes, but Aubrey isn't forward enough to admit it, so she sits still, blinking repeatedly.

Despite Aubrey's silence, Daniel does not feel rejected. Instead, he keeps speaking. "The only reason I'm here is to talk to you … figure out why you make me smile so much."

Aubrey can feel her heart trying to expand in her chest, but something is restricting it, causing it to malfunction. She wants to tell him she is there for him too, but she can only smile. Daniel smiles in return. They sit face-to-face grinning at each other. "Okay, well, let's talk," Aubrey utters, turning toward him and resting her cheek in her palm.

Daniel leans in as well. "Your ex-boyfriend. What happened?" he asks, coming out blazing.

All the tingles disperse. Aubrey sits up and leans away. "Let me guess, Travis has been dragging my name?"

"He did bring it up. I'm only bringing it up to draw my own conclusions about you."

Aubrey sits quietly for a long moment before deciding to respond. "Well, first of all, he was never my boyfriend. We were friends, and the friendship just didn't work," she answers vaguely. "Why are you running track when you're one of the best football players in the nation?" She throws the heat right back at him.

Daniel stills himself, preparing to politely tackle the question he despises. It wasn't anyone's business why his life was on a different path. It irritated him that people had the audacity to ask. But he decides to be tactful about it with Aubrey. "I had a lot going on with my family, so..." He doesn't finish the sentence. Aubrey waits for the rest of his statement while Daniel waits for her to move on. The two of them sit in awkward silence.

After a moment, Aubrey breaks the silence with an uneasy chuckle. "This conversation isn't going well."

"You're right." He sighs. Daniel is annoyed with himself for initiating the battle of questions. Talking to women before was never a problem. He struggles to fathom why Aubrey's company has him entirely frazzled. "I'm trying too hard. I should have kept it basic and asked you where you grew up?"

Aubrey wags her head from side to side. "That question will lead to questions about family, and my family isn't a lovely topic."

Dropping his face into his hands, Daniel growls out a low laugh at how horribly their talk unfolds. He makes a last-ditch effort. "Favorite color?"

"Blue." Aubrey giggles. "What's your major?" Aubrey asks, optimistic that they can get it together.

Daniel slowly lifts his head, giving her an apologetic look. "Engineering is my major, but I am doing it for my parents. Getting a *worthwhile* degree is a religion to them," he explains. "I'm going to finish the degree, but my focus is on making it to the NFL and using that platform to make a difference. What about you?

"I'm unsure about my future. That's why I chose CSU. I love how the curriculum focuses more on helping people discover themselves first. I heard about the mentors and knew it was exactly what I needed. So that's my goal right now ... figuring out how to show up as the best version of myself, and then I'll apply that to a career."

"I think that's amazing," Daniel praises.

Daniel relaxes his legs, feeling good because they have finally begun a good conversation. Then, inadvertently, his knee touches Aubrey's. She jerks away, crossing her legs and arms, shielding herself from his infiltration.

The conversation is hijacked by Jade, who boldly sits down. "Surprised to see you here, Aubrey. I never see you at social gatherings."

Jade doesn't like how Aubrey walks around like she is superior to everyone else. Aubrey has no problem with Jade but grasps that she isn't Jade's favorite person. Unfortunately, one woman's confidence can lead to another woman's insecurity. Choosing not to entertain the spitefulness, Aubrey simply shrugs one shoulder.

"I invited Daniel over for a small after-party. You should come too," Jade continues, trying to get a reaction from her.

"No thanks, but y'all have fun." Aubrey stands and walks away. Daniel grabs the plate of food from the table and tosses it in a nearby trash. He follows behind Aubrey. Jade watches the two of them walk away, her head seemingly getting longer with each step they take.

Aubrey approaches Lily and hugs her. "I'm heading home. Please let me know when you're home safely."

Lily responds with a military salute, and Aubrey proceeds toward the exit. Daniel takes a moment to say bye to Travis and thank him for the invite before leaving. When he gets to his car, he spots Aubrey in her car. She turns her key, firing up the engine but the engine stutters. Aubrey tries it again, ending with the same lifeless results. She turns the key over and over, making the engine cough. Daniel approaches her car and knocks on the window. She rolls down the glass slightly, leaving a crack in the opening. "That's not helping," he tells her.

"I can see that," she replies, rolling up her window and stepping out of the car. "On your way to the after-party?"

"I was never going," he says, spreading his full lips into a breathtaking smile. "Why? Are you feeling possessive of me, like I'm your man?"

Rolling her eyes, Aubrey walks to the back of her car, opening the trunk. She hides her embarrassment by exposing that she cares if Daniel spends the evening with Jade.

"Do you have jumper cables in there? If not, I can give you a ride home, and we can figure out your car when we have more daylight."

Aubrey looks at the jumper cables sprawled out in her trunk, then looks up at Daniel, standing by the front of her car. She desires more time with him. She closes the trunk, deciding to take advantage of the opportunity. "I'll accept the ride. Thank you."

Chapter Four

THE MOMENT Aubrey sits in Daniel's car, she regrets her decision. His smell is a thousand times more potent, making her feel like she is in a dream. Goosebumps arise on her skin. She hugs herself and rubs her arms, willing the goosebumps away.

"Are you cold?" Daniel touches the car screen to turn down the air conditioning.

"I'm fine," Aubrey replies, even though *fine* isn't an accurate description of her feelings.

"You sure?" he asks again, noticing her discomfort.

"I'm sure."

Keeping one hand on the steering wheel, Daniel reaches his other hand over to rest it on the back of the passenger seat. It is his usual way of driving because he does it absentmindedly. Still, it doesn't stop Aubrey from inching away from him.

Daniel thinks of how she reacted when his knee touched her. He pulls his hand away, wanting her to feel safe in his company.

"I want you to know I didn't mean to put my leg against yours earlier. I wouldn't come at you like that," he professes with genuine care.

Aubrey releases her hold on herself, letting her arms fall comfortably in her lap. "I discerned that." A small piece of Aubrey wishes that he had come at her incorrectly to ruin her affection for him. She doesn't necessarily enjoy having feelings for a man. It is confusing, time-consuming, and exhausting. "Do you know how people say they can hear or smell everything?"

Daniel nods.

"Well, I can feel everything—love, hate, joy, sadness. So, I don't like people touching me because I don't want to feel."

"Wow, that's kinda deep. But I understand."

Quietness takes over as they process the moment. Finally, Daniel turns on some music when the silence becomes uncomfortable. The melody drifts through the speakers. Daniel hums along and sways with the beat. It is a popular song that has been playing on every radio station and will likely become the choice song for the wedding season. "You like this song?" Daniel asks.

Aubrey shrugs carelessly. Although she doesn't love the song, Aubrey doesn't dislike it either. "I guess I can get into a sad love song just as much as the next person."

Daniel's mouth falls open. He loves the song. "You think this song is sad?"

"It is," she replies matter-of-factly. She touches the screen to bump up the volume. "Listen to her. She's so in love it's painful. Her heart aches for him when he's not around. When he is near, she needs him to be

29

touching her. She just said she can't breathe when she's with him. Why can't she breathe? Shouldn't love have the opposite effect?"

Her opinion evokes a snicker from Daniel. "She's passionate and in love," he defends. "Are you telling me you don't want passionate love?"

"I don't want anything that gives me anxiety."

Daniel takes a moment to examine her eyes, unsuccessfully trying to figure her out. "Your ex-boyfriend broke your heart, didn't he," Daniel guesses.

"He was not my boyfriend, and why are we still talking about him?"

"I'm just trying to figure you out."

Aubrey doesn't have an explanation to offer him since she is still trying to figure herself out. Then, thankfully, his phone starts ringing, distracting him. The words *Big Sis* flash across his screen, and Daniel declines the call before it can ring fully.

"You can talk to your sister," Aubrey encourages.

"I'm talking to you," he says.

As Daniel finishes his sentence, another call comes in from his sister. Daniel declines again and powers off his phone. "She doesn't want anything."

"We're home anyway, so…" Aubrey says, pointing out they are around the corner from the dorm building. Both their expressions turn forlorn, missing each other before they separate. "Thank you for the ride."

"Anytime, Aubrey." Her name glides off his lips like it belongs there.

The moment Daniel puts his car in park, Aubrey steps out of the car and starts talking to God inwardly. *Um, why does this man live next door to me? You gotta be testing me! Or did the ancient serpent himself send him to me to distract me?* Aubrey eyes Daniel with more scrutiny as they step onto the elevator. He is beaming with joy. *Joy doesn't come from the ancient serpent;* she rationalizes her doubts. Aubrey decides that the smart thing to do is control her feelings until he consistently displays joy, love, peace, patience, goodness, kindness, gentleness, self-control, faithfulness, chastity, modesty, and perseverance.

The elevator doors open. Daniel and Aubrey walk to their doors. "Hey," Daniel calls before entering his apartment.

Aubrey looks over to find his bottom lip sucked into his mouth and euphoria in his eyes. Daniel awaits her response, but his handsomeness arrests her breath. "Hmm?" she manages to utter.

"I saw those jumper cables in your trunk."

Aubrey suppresses the urge to run inside her apartment to hide her mortification. "What? What are you talking about?" The gigantic smile covering her face gives her away as she opens the door and disappears.

Chuckling, Daniel turns the doorknob and walks into his apartment. Once inside, he finds his sister sitting on his sofa. She has one leg crossed over the other, bouncing it impatiently. She glares at him as he sets his keys and phone on the end table. "So, you do have your phone?" Kennedy demands. "And you turned it off."

"I'm a grown man. I don't have to answer you."

Without speaking a word, Kennedy starts aggressively tapping her phone screen. Ringing comes from the speakerphone.

"Hello?" a tired voice answers.

"I found him, Mom," Kennedy says.

"Daniel?" His mom speaks his name as if he is in trouble.

Daniel sits on the sofa beside Kennedy, bumping her out of the way and taking the phone. "Sylvia Sane! What's up, girl?" he asks playfully. Daniel is the baby in the family and his mom's favorite. He has always been able to win her over with humor and love. "I miss you."

"Miss you too," she replies, sweetness in her tone. "How was your evening? What did you get into?"

"I had a great evening. How about you? How's traveling going?"

"You didn't answer my question," she points out. "What did you get into?"

The playful demeanor starts to fade. "I didn't get into anything, Mom."

"Your sister said you went to a party, and she couldn't contact you."

Daniel glances at Kennedy, annoyed. He slowly shakes his head from side to side, shaming her. "It was a barbeque, not a party."

"That university gave you a second chance to finish your education," she chastises sternly. "You are there with one goal, which is to improve yourself. You don't have time for a party, a barbeque, or whatever you want to call it. Do you hear me?"

"I hear you, Mom."

"I'll call you later. I love you."

The call ends before Daniel can say the words, *love you too*. He hands Kennedy her phone without looking at her.

"You didn't answer my calls," Kennedy exclaims, guilt heavy in her tone.

"Do you know how hurtful it is for my family to treat me like this? I get it. I messed up, but I'm not checking in with my sister whenever I go somewhere."

"We just worry about you."

Daniel huffs out a long groan. "I know. But it's time to move on. I'm done living like this."

EVEN ON SATURDAY mornings, Aubrey climbs out of bed at four a.m. Early rising became a habit once she felt the undisputed peace from morning stillness. With bare feet, she quietly moves across the cold wooden floor. She opens her blinds to let in the street lighting until the rising sun replaces them. Striking a lighter against her candle wick, the flickering adds a calming glow and the aroma of lavender. Shadows of herself cast against the empty white walls as she stretches her body, feeling it awaken with each movement. Eventually, she stops moving and sits entirely still, inhaling and exhaling. She begins going through her day in her head, mapping out everything down to the minor details—even what she plans to eat for a snack. As she thinks through the day, she sees smooth dark skin, deep brown eyes, and plump lips surrounded by perfectly trimmed chin hairs. Whenever his face appears in her mind, she opens her eyes to refocus her meditation. The moment her lids drop again, his face comes flooding back. Her eyes fly open, and she drops her head into her hands, raking her fingers through her hair. She stands, abandoning her morning routine. She takes a long shower, eats breakfast, and laces up her sneakers. She walks out of the apartment building and starts the five-mile run to campus.

The wind blowing across her face and through her hair is exhilarating. When she runs, she feels powerful and in control. Sometimes her body would want to give up, but she mastered how to keep going until she accomplished what she set out to do. Every run gives her confidence that she will one day conquer her heart the way she dominates her body. She stops to freshen up when she reaches the indoor arena before heading to the campus library. When she walks in, she sees Daniel drenched in sweat. He is sprinting down the turf as if football scouts are watching him. He runs with his fists balled up, jaw clenched, and stiff arms. It is some of the ugliest running she has ever witnessed. Daniel drops to his knees and hangs his head when he finishes running. Aubrey can see the mental agony torturing him.

She walks toward him. Feeling her presence, he looks up. A smile stretches over his face. It is a façade. "Good morning," she greets.

"Hey," he replies, pushing himself to his feet. "How'd you get here?"

"My two legs work pretty well. I'm a runner," she reminds him with a sarcastic smile.

Daniel doesn't find her humor funny at all. "It's early for you to be running by yourself."

Aubrey waves off his concern. "A squad of angels protects me everywhere I go."

"Well, I'm joining the squad." Daniel picks up his phone from the sideline. "Send me your location."

"I don't know you like that," Aubrey rebuts jokingly.

"Please?" he asks with fervent resolve. "To make sure you're safe."

Aubrey feels her heart trying to expand again. She can't comprehend why someone she barely knows would care about her safety when her mother doesn't care to check on her. Pulling her phone from her leggings pocket, she opens it up. "What's your number?"

They exchange numbers and locations. "Thank you," Daniel says, his eyes deep and genuine.

Aubrey feels the heat increasing in her cheeks, adoring how he looks at her. "What are you up to?" she asks, distracting her thoughts.

Daniel sighs. "I'm out of shape. I need to get it together if I want an invite to the Scouting Combine," he explains. "I need to get my forty-meter time down, lose some fat, gain some muscle ... everything really."

"Why not play football?" she inquires. "It doesn't make sense for you to be on the track team."

"Umm." He looks down at the turf, then back up at Aubrey, caution apparent in his eyes. "Football starts in the summer. I was unavailable in the summer, so I missed the opportunity to play. It's my senior year, and I needed to do something. Coach Aaron graciously allowed me to participate even though the season had already started, so here I am."

Nodding slowly, Aubrey registers his words without understanding them. It takes everything inside her not to ask why he was unavailable in the summer. A voice inside tells her to mind her business. "You're working too hard," she says.

Daniel's brows pull together. "What do you mean?"

"You're tense when you run. You should relax and let your form do the work for you." Aubrey pumps her arms to demonstrate. She is hardly moving but looks powerful.

"Can you teach me?"

"I can put you on my schedule," she states. "I have somewhere to be right now."

Daniel turns his wrist to check his watch. "Yeah, I have somewhere to be also. But I'm free to start tomorrow if you are?"

"Tomorrow morning," Aubrey tells him and exits the arena.

She walks to the campus library and stops at the door displaying a sign that reads *Mental Success Group*. When she enters, the smell of eucalyptus and the sound of the ocean offers instant relaxation. Sunlight pours in through oversized windows, providing plenty of light to satiate the healthy fiddle leaf fig tree in the corner. Fourteen ecru beanbag chairs make up a circle in the middle of the room. Each chair has a cozy white blanket and pillow to accompany it. Aubrey kicks off her shoes and eagerly enters the space. A young man with blue eyes and blond curls greets her from the middle of the circle. "Good to see you, Aubrey! How are you?" he welcomes enthusiastically.

"Hey, Adam. I'm doing great," Aubrey answers, matching his enthusiasm. She sinks into one of the beanbag chairs and exhales. As she settles in, she hears a familiar voice in the back of the room. She whips her head around to check if it's exactly who she thinks. Daniel walks in, and Adam greets him like they are old friends. Aubrey's mouth hangs open, shocked to have Daniel in the place where she is most vulnerable. Aubrey selfishly wants to keep it as her own haven.

Internally, she knows Daniel can benefit from being part of a mental success group. Everybody needs it.

Donning an exuberant smile Daniel picks up an empty bean bag and places it beside her, "I think you're following me."

Chapter Five

"YOU ARE NOT in this group!" Aubrey states, astounded.

"I am. Adam is my mentor," Daniel explains.

"How?" Aubrey says more harshly than she intends.

Daniel flashes a patient smile. "Everybody is assigned a mentor at this university, right?"

"Yes, but he's my assigned mentor."

"Small world. I guess you'll see me at home, practice, and now in the group."

As the words come out of Daniel's mouth, they look at each other, thinking the same thing—why are their lives aligning so perfectly?

"Seems like all of creation is conspiring to make us friends."

"And your arms are too short to box with God, so don't fight it."

Daniel's statement is so corny and cute at the same time, Aubrey cannot help but smile. They permit themselves a moment to withdraw from reality in each other's gaze.

"Daniel Sane!" a guy pops his head into their conversation, causing them to jump. "I just wanted to tell you that I watched all your games. I've never seen anyone catch like you. You're amazing!"

"Appreciate that, man."

Daniel and Aubrey watch the guy bounce excitedly to his beanbag chair.

"How does it feel to have everyone know who you are?" Aubrey asks.

"It's a double-edged sword. When you're doing good, everyone showers you with love. But, when you make a mistake, you deactivate your social media and hide under a rock."

Aubrey stares at him, wanting to pull out her phone and type his name into a search engine.

"I needed something to knock me off my high horse, though," he continues. "I loved the glory and notoriety too much. Next time, I'll do it correctly and be more purposeful."

Aubrey replies with a slow, suspicious nod.

Adam stands in the middle of the circle and begins class by saying the exact words he always says whenever there is a newcomer. "As always, we are going to discuss—not argue or debate but have a respectful discussion. Today, I want to discuss the statement, *People Need People*. Do you believe people indeed need other people?"

Aubrey's hand and Daniel's hands go up at the same time. Adam nods in Aubrey's direction, letting her know the space is hers.

"I don't believe that people need other people. We desire others. However, everything each person needs is already inside of them. If someone decides to abandon someone or not help them, it doesn't mean that person won't survive."

Adam thanks Aubrey for adding to the discussion and nods toward Daniel.

"Of course, anyone can survive alone, but people thrive when they have others. Something as simple as a touch..." Daniel reaches out and gently strokes Aubrey's arm with the back of his finger. His example resonates perfectly because his quick touch arouses every part of Aubrey. "...or a hug in the morning can change someone's day for the better. People need people ... to love and care for and be there for them."

Aubrey picks up on the tenderness in his tone. It is evident to her that he comes from a loving home. "What about the people who don't grow up getting hugs and kisses? Are they lacking something? Are they not thriving? What becomes of them?" Aubrey blurts out, triggered.

"The beautiful thing about life is you get to choose what you become," Daniel replies calmly. "It doesn't matter how someone is raised; there comes a time in every person's life when they get to raise themselves. And there is never a moment where anyone is too old for hugs and kisses."

The discussion follows Aubrey and Daniel out the door. "I really enjoyed that," Daniel says as they walk across campus.

"Mm hmm," Aubrey replies. She had been quietly reflective throughout the rest of the discussion.

"So, were you talking about yourself in class? Are you someone who doesn't need others?"

Aubrey stops walking to overthink his words. Did she come off as cold? "Why are you asking me that?"

"Well, from what I've picked up on so far and from what I've? heard, you don't let people get close to you."

"From what you've? heard?" Aubrey rolls her eyes and starts walking again. "You need to stop listening to Travis."

"He's a friend. I prayed to find a good friend here."

"What is your definition of a friend?" she challenges.

"Someone like-minded, driven, and likes to stay lowkey."

Aubrey laughs. "So, which one of those qualities fits Travis?"

Daniel joins her laughter. "I'm not sure. Maybe the friend I prayed for is in a package I didn't expect. Maybe he is a she." Daniel wiggles his brows at Aubrey, driving his point home.

Aubrey smiles. "This friend doesn't come with benefits."

"Aww! Should've been more specific with my prayers," he jokes.

A slight smirk graces her face, finding him amusing. "What else did you pray for?" Aubrey inquires as she stops on the student union's steps.

Daniel points up the steps. "Are you heading to lunch too? If so, I can tell you over lunch."

Aubrey looks up the steps at the crowd of students flowing through the union. She remembers how their teammates had looked at them when they walked into the weight room together. She is also aware that people knew they left the cookout simultaneously. Travis was already spreading false news about her. If they ate lunch together, she imagines what rumors would circulate. "Uhm, I don't know if a public lunch is a good idea. I don't want people thinking I'm with you."

Daniel's brows shoot up to the top of his face. "What's wrong with me?"

Aubrey smiles sweetly. "You're amazing, Daniel. But I prefer discretion. I don't like everybody in my business, and too many people know who you are."

Daniel chuckles. "Okay, well, we can have lunch at home. I'll cook. We can finish our conversation, and nobody will ever know we had lunch together."

Aubrey searches his eyes, checking his intentions and wondering if it is a good idea to go into his apartment. "Don't say home like we live together," Aubrey refutes.

Daniel starts laughing while raising his hands innocently. "Seems like you want to establish some boundaries. I'm not trying to do anything but eat lunch and be your friend."

Aubrey searches his eyes for a moment longer. Deciding to trust him, she descends the steps and starts toward his car. "And you better know how to cook," she adds, while shooting a playful smile in his direction.

AUBREY TAKES ONE STEP inside Daniel's apartment and starts giggling. The comparison of his apartment to her apartment is literally comical. It doesn't seem like they live on the same planet, let alone in the same building. "What's funny?" Daniel asks.

"I did not expect a college student to be living like this. This looks like a staged model home." Aubrey kicks off her shoes out of respect for his plush throw rug.

"My sister decorated. Kennedy is an interior designer," he explains.

Aubrey walks over to his photo gallery wall and delves deeper into his life. A photo of Daniel as a little boy resting on his sister's hip makes her smile. "How much older is your sister than you?"

"Only five years, but she acts like a third parent."

Aubrey can hear a softness in his voice that conveys appreciation for his sister. She moves on to the next photo. Daniel's parents are on the beach in their wedding attire. Their smiles are big and luminous. They seem joyful and deeply in love. She continues reviewing the photos while Daniel moves to the kitchen to prepare lunch.

"Anything in particular you want?" he asks.

"I eat cereal for breakfast, lunch, and dinner, so..." She doesn't finish her sentence. She is too busy looking at a photo of Kennedy and Daniel's mother. The two women are stunning, classy, and serene. They are side by side with identical eyes. Aubrey starts feeling a tugging on her heart and moisture in her eyes, so she looks away. Her gaze lands on Daniel. He is staring at her with a peculiar expression. He didn't miss the moment she just had. "What are my options?" she asks to divert his focus.

"I can make you my signature salmon dish?"

"Sounds perfect."

Aubrey doesn't look away from him, and Daniel doesn't dare take his eyes away from her. It is all it takes for them to be grinning at each other again.

"Aren't you going to start cooking?" Aubrey questions.

Daniel takes a few more seconds to take her in before opening the refrigerator and taking out the ingredients. "Do you honestly eat cereal for breakfast, lunch, and dinner?"

"Sometimes I eat at the student union."

Daniel slowly shakes his head, feigning disappointment. "Well, it sounds like I just found myself a lunch buddy. I can't have you eating like that. You're an athlete," he states, inviting himself to spend even more time with her.

Aubrey welcomes his invitation. "I would love that."

Sitting on his leather couch, Aubrey brings her knees to her chest, making herself comfortable. As she sits back, she notices a face-down photo on his end table. She has an instant urge to pick it up. From the corner of her eye, Aubrey looks at Daniel and sees that he is busy cooking, so she lets her curiosity have its way. Aubrey picks up the photo, scanning over it. It is a photo of a woman. The woman's smile is familiar, but it takes Aubrey a moment to recognize the woman as Daniel's mother, even though Aubrey has just finished looking at several pictures of her. His mother weighs about fifty pounds less than all the other photos. It doesn't appear that she has any hair. There is a sunken and dark look in her eyes. Aubrey looks up, and this time Daniel is watching her. He isn't smiling. The usual glimmer in his eye is gone. Rather, he looks like a shell of a man, as if his spirit is dormant and needs to be reawakened.

Aubrey puts the photo back on the end table, laying it face down like before. "Your family is beautiful."

He responds with a weak smile. "You wanted to know what else I prayed for, remember?" Daniel reminds her, changing the subject.

"Yep. Tell me." Aubrey leans in, eager to learn more about him.

"I prayed for a mentor for personal growth. I got Adam."

"Adam is great."

"He is. I like him a lot."

"I'm glad."

Daniel nods and continues. "I prayed for someone to help me get back in shape, so I can get an invite to the NFL combine."

"I don't know much about football, but I know about speed. So I'll help you until the right person comes along."

Daniel's eyes travel over her body, noticing how beautifully fit she is. He is in good hands. "I can't express how much I appreciate that," he professes.

Aubrey waves off his gratitude. "It is my pleasure," she responds casually.

Daniel's lips spread over his white teeth as he gazes at Aubrey with admiration and gratefulness. Aubrey feels her heart starting to hope, but she quickly blocks it. She doesn't trust hope.

"Is the food finished yet?" she asks to distract herself, dodging every possible feeling that tries to infiltrate her.

Daniel looks down at the salmon searing in the skillet. He puts it onto a plate with asparagus and rice, drizzling everything with a sweet chili glaze. "Bon appétit."

They sit next to each other in front of the small kitchen island, eating the lunch Daniel had prepared. Aubrey dances and moans after each bite, providing a show for Daniel. He enjoys every second of her entertainment. Finally, when nothing but crumbs are left, she relaxes back in her seat and exhales. "Who taught you how to cook like that?"

"The one and only Sylvia Sane. My mama," he replies proudly.

Aubrey reads the endearment written all over his face. "You and your mom are close." It isn't a question. The answer is apparent.

"She's my best friend," Daniel states in an almost inaudible tone.

Aubrey doesn't know what to say, so she doesn't say anything. Instead, they sit still and quietly, letting the moment sink in.

"What's up with your mom?" Daniel asks unexpectedly.

Aubrey opens her mouth to speak, but no sound comes out. She mashes her lips together and again says nothing.

"I just want to know you," Daniel insists softly.

"Nothing's up. We aren't close anymore," she blurts out.

"Well, what happened?" Daniel asks hard questions straightforwardly, expecting to get an answer. He waits as Aubrey nervously chews on the corner of her lip.

Aubrey matches Daniel's penetrating eyes, pondering if she will dismiss the question or grant him access to one of her most aching inner wounds. She continues studying his attentive expression. He wants her to tell him badly, and she wants to unbury her pain just as much to have someone understand her. No one had cared enough in the past to ask about her life. People usually judge her as cold and unfriendly, which isn't entirely false. Nevertheless, she wants someone to care. She needs someone. The desire for intimacy overpowers her reluctance.

"The last time I saw my mom, I was sixteen," she begins. Closing her eyes, the memories flood her mind. She could see the beautiful two-story home with the immaculate lawn. Of course, her mother was on her knees, replacing the weeds with colorful flowers. "My mom loved that house," Aubrey tells Daniel. "She took pride in making it a home."

Aubrey remembers rollerblading up the driveway that day while her mother watched with a proud smile. It is one of Aubrey's favorite memories of her mother because her mom looked at her with so much love. Aubrey can still see the smile as if it happened five minutes ago instead of five years ago. "She hugged me so tightly. Some days I can literally still feel that embrace." Aubrey exhales a peaceful sigh as the feeling comforts her at that moment. "After she hugged me, the smile faded from her face. She asked me if I was happy. In the past five years, I have connected the dots that I didn't understand then. Something was going on with her boyfriend. He wasn't normally a bad person, but he started acting differently. I can recall the looks he gave me. I'm sure my mom was trying to protect me. I just can't figure out why she got rid of me and not him." Aubrey stops talking to think over the situation for what feels like the millionth time. Her expression twists as she racks her brain for understanding. Eventually, she quits trying to understand and accepts the situation for what it is.

"I ran to Lily's house," Aubrey continues. "A few days later, Lily's mom told me she talked to my mom, and they decided I would finish high school living with Lily's family. I called her every day for a month straight. I just wanted to talk to figure out what was happening. She never answered or returned my calls. That was five years ago. She still hasn't called, emailed, shown up to a track meet … nothing. Then, one day after I got my driver's license and car, I crept by the house. Like always, she was working on the lawn, and something in me broke. I couldn't understand how she could go about her normal routine without me. We were inseparable," she says, her voice beginning to shake. "I thought we were inseparable. Turned out, I didn't really know her like that at all." Her emotions overwhelm her, so she stops talking to avoid crying.

"Your vulnerability is the most beautiful thing I've ever seen," Daniel marvels through a whisper. "Thank you for not hiding from me."

Aubrey's hand gravitates to her belly, holding herself from collapsing into his lap. She didn't know how much she needed someone to create a safe space where she didn't need to hide. His care for her triggers more emotion. Aubrey forces her lips to curve up into a counterfeit smile. Then, she reverts to hiding. "Well, that's my story. Your turn. What did you do? What caused you to miss the football season?"

Daniel's brows raise high on his forehead, and his eyes go blank as he thinks about how to deny Aubrey access to that season of his life. He wasn't that person anymore. In fact, he was working hard to kill that person so no one could ever access him again. A long moment of silence passes as Aubrey waits, and Daniel chooses his words carefully.

"I just want to know you." Aubrey giggles, finding humor in using his own words against him.

"I'm not him anymore; I don't want you to know that person. I want you to know the man sitting beside you right now."

Aubrey folds her arms over her chest. "So, why'd you have me digging up my past if you never planned to unbury yours?"

Daniel winces, feeling the heat of Aubrey's disappointment. He regrets asking her the question. "I realize now that I shouldn't have asked you to do that. I apologize." Daniel internally chastises himself for getting into the situation. Part of him wants to tell her just to gain her trust. But he worries that he'd gain her judgment instead—that she'd become another person in addition to his family that sees him as weak and uncontrolled. He can't risk it.

Aubrey's brown eyes narrow into suspicious slits as she watches Daniel drag his hand across his forehead, seeming to struggle internally. He looks distressed, and she can't fathom what is causing his anguish. Whatever it is, she doesn't care enough to ask any more questions. "I'm going to go." She stands and walks toward the door, sliding her feet into her shoes. "Thanks for lunch. It was delicious."

"Lunch again tomorrow?" he asks, hopeful.

Turning the doorknob, Aubrey opens the door and walks out, ignoring his invitation.

"What about your car? I can take you to it." He tries again.

"I'll walk. It's not that far."

"Please don't be mad at me," he pleads.

"I'm not mad," she throws out over her shoulder before closing the door. She lies. There is fury in her heart. She feels exposed … naked … raw. How dare he

49

allow her to reveal her secrets if he didn't intend to do the same?

Once back in her space, she takes out her laptop, opens the search engine, and types in Daniel Sane. He is a well-known football player who made a big enough mistake to get kicked out of a Division I college. His pseudo-celebrity status is reason enough to make his shortcomings national news.

Chapter Six

AUBREY'S EYES EAGERLY scan over the laptop screen, reading every word about Daniel. After hours of reading, she only discovers his birthplace, that he maintained straight A's in school, and that his father is a surgeon who invented a medical device used at every American hospital. There is just one article that addresses his departure from football. It doesn't have any concrete information. Instead, the article includes speculation about a possible injury.

Determined to discover his secret, Aubrey moves from Google to paying money to run a background check on him. He doesn't have a criminal record, not even a traffic violation. Next, she searches his social media pages, scanning through years and years of his profile. She looks through his friends' profiles when she doesn't find what she wants on his profile. She still doesn't see what she's looking for. After an exhausting three-hour effort, she closes her laptop, concluding that his skeletons are buried too deep to find.

THE NEXT MORNING, Aubrey leaves her apartment early to avoid running into Daniel in front of the elevator. She jogs to Travis' house and subjects herself to asking for his assistance in jump starting her car. Travis obliges Aubrey with minimal resistance. She drives to campus earlier than usual. The campus is practically empty. Taking advantage of the morning serenity, Aubrey sits directly in the sun at one of the picnic tables. Feeling the warmth touch her skin, she closes her eyes, wrapping herself in her arms while breathing in and out slowly and steadily. After ten minutes of breathing, a familiar voice breaks her stillness.

"What up, cupcake? Long time no see."

She doesn't have to open her eyes to know it's Jace—the man she had been hiding from for the past six months. His rough and urban tone is somewhat melodic to her ears. Just hearing his voice brings back fun memories of their friendship. She remembers dancing with him at halftime during the college basketball games. Jace would invite her to stand and dance to whatever song would come on. He asked so many times that she finally conceded. It was an exhilarating feeling to dance and not care who was watching. She recalls their late nights eating French fries dipped in chocolate ice cream. Even though they were friends, both started seeing each other as more. They had a mutual attraction and connection. Jace was like the forbidden fruit that Aubrey knew she shouldn't touch.

He is the opposite of Daniel—more rugged, whereas Daniel is polished. Jace curses every other word; Daniel only speaks excellence. Jace's body is covered in tattoos; Daniel let God's creation speak for itself. Jace is conceited about his good looks; Daniel is confident while being self-aware about what he can improve. Jace will be the perfect mate for some woman someday, but Aubrey knows she isn't that woman. Still, something about Jace excites Aubrey and makes her feel invincible. She opens her eyes to acknowledge him but can't find adequate words to express her conflicting feelings once their gazes meet.

"Don't tell me you're still not talking to me," Jace says when she doesn't respond.

"How are you, Jace?" Aubrey asks politely and professionally, practicing self-control.

"I'm good. Don't I look good?" He smiles widely. Aubrey rolls her eyes. Jace is aware of how appealing he is, and he is arrogant about it. "Don't be shy about it. We both know what this is."

Despite her best intentions, she laughs. "Still prince charming."

"I'm just missing my princess," he throws out the bait.

"Aww. Can't find any willing candidates?" Aubrey dodges his hook.

"Plenty willing, but only one worthy of the position."

"Too bad. If only you were looking for a queen." Knots begin forming in her stomach. She had already experienced how one casual conversation with Jace could turn into a yearlong love affair. She picks up her backpack and slides it over her shoulder. "I need to get going, but it was good seeing you," she says, standing from the table.

Jace doesn't acknowledge her attempt to leave. He is unwilling to let her go so easily after waiting so long to see her. Instead, he stands in front of her, wearing the smuggest expression.

"Why are you looking at me like that?" she asks instead of walking away.

"Because you didn't mention Mr. Football, who I've heard you've been hanging out with. He must not be your boyfriend. So, I still have a chance with you."

Aubrey begins fiddling with her backpack straps, uncomfortable because she knows they have unfinished business. She is still trying to figure out a tactful way to finish it. "I gotta go," she says again and starts walking off.

"You just disappeared on me," Jace calls out, continuing the conversation even though she is walking away. "Ghosted me. I thought we were better than that."

Aubrey stops walking to turn back and face him. "It was me, not you." She delivers the cliché line knowing that it isn't a valid explanation.

"How long you gonna keep running? Let's handle this like adults. I mean, that's what a *queen* would do, right?"

Aubrey's brown eyes turn big and round as she stares up at him, full of uncertainty. Aubrey wishes she could reasonably explain why she ghosted him, but she can't. All she knows is that she entered a season of self-growth and improvement, which required her to distance herself from Jace. "I'll call you," she lies, then turns around and quickly retreats.

After the encounter with Jace, Aubrey walks into track practice even more resolved about staying away from Daniel. One of the main reasons that she broke things off with Jace was to have mental clarity while on her journey of personal development. So what makes Daniel any different? Aubrey decides to stay away from Daniel for good ... but then he enters the arena. His presence overpowers her resolve. She keeps telling herself to look away from him, but her eyes won't listen. Before she knows it, he walks toward her, wearing his typical grin. In an attempt to avoid him, Aubrey starts her warm-up stretching routine.

"Hey, hey," Daniel greets, falling in sync with her stretches.

"I googled you last night," Aubrey confronts, not wanting to beat around the bush. "Even ran a background check and stalked your social media."

Daniel chuckles, confident that there isn't anything on the Internet about his situation. "Did you at least follow me while stalking my social media?"

As they are talking, Coach walks by with folded arms. He gives them a stern look, causing Daniel and Aubrey to do more stretching and less talking. Once Coach is past them, Aubrey stops stretching to keep talking. "Did you accost someone?" she probes.

Daniel's easygoing humor quickly fades. "What?"

"Murder? Manslaughter? Embezzlement?" she continues without remorse.

"Do you honestly think I'm capable of doing any of those things?"

Before Aubrey can open her mouth to answer, Coach calls their names. "Aubrey Blake and Daniel Sane, this is your warning. If you keep talking, you'll be doing extra work."

Aubrey and Daniel nod to acknowledge his warning. The moment Coach turns his back, Aubrey starts conversing again. "I don't know you at all because you won't tell me."

"Why do you want to know me by my mistakes?"

Daniel challenges.

Aubrey struggles to come up with an adequate response. He has asked a fair question. She racks her brain for a rebuttal while studying Daniel's expression. He silently pleads with Aubrey as if he wants her to give him the benefit of the doubt. Aubrey isn't the kind of person who ignores signs. She believes people when they show her who they are.

"Just get to know me and then decide who I am," he requests.

Aubrey quietly analyzes him, pondering if it's worth it. He isn't asking for much. All he wants is a fair judgment of him based on his current actions, not his past. Unable to deny that his request is rational, Aubrey shrugs easily. "I already committed to helping you," she says, giving any excuse to avoid admitting that he is right and she is wrong. "Besides, we're teammates, neighbors, and group mates. Getting to know you seems inevitable."

A triumphant smile stretches across his face. "Well, let that be the reason."

Coach steps in front of them, his fist on his hip and his brows pulled together. "I warned y'all. Now I need one hundred standing twist crunches."

"Kay," Aubrey accepts, knowing she deserves it. She begins taking off her warm-up clothes, preparing for her punishment as if it was nothing. "And I apologize, Coach," she offers sweetly.

"Yeah, we apologize, and we're finished talking," Daniel adds more pleadingly, hoping Coach will change his mind.

"Appreciate the apology. Now, let's get it." Coach pushes a button on his portable speaker, and a beat drops.

Aubrey twists her torso, jumping to one side and

bringing her knee into a crunch. Daniel reluctantly follows suit. Coach watches them do a few reps before walking away to tend to the rest of the team.

"We have one hundred of these!" Daniel huffs, winded already.

"Try to focus on the music, not the pain," Aubrey advises.

Daniel twists into a jump, on beat with the music, and adds a little dance.

"There you go," Aubrey encourages through a giggle.

Coach turns around to check on them, and Daniel straightens up and does his twist crunches normally. When Coach looks away, Daniel starts dancing again, his arms and facial expressions extremely animated. Aubrey watches him dance, entertained and amused by his moves. He is a great dancer and a beautiful distraction for Aubrey. Coach checks in after a while and asks Aubrey how many they've done since he trusts her to tell the truth.

"Sixty-seven," she tells Coach, containing her laughter to avoid exposing Daniel. She extends more energy than she intends, playing around with Daniel. On rep seventy-five, she starts feeling the burn and slows down.

"Add in a little dance," Daniel suggests, leading by example. Aubrey falls in rhythm with him, mimicking his moves. "Yeaaahhhh!" Daniel gasses her up. They finish their remaining reps, dancing together and laughing freely as if they are old friends.

When practice ends, Daniel and Aubrey lounge on the track, exhausted from their extra work. Daniel opens his bag and pulls out a leather book engraved with the words Life Plan on the front. He also takes out a pen and opens the book, confidently showing Aubrey his list of goals.

"You carry this with you everywhere you go?" Aubrey questions.

"I'm intentional about what I want in life. I plan to get everything I want." Daniel gives her a look to let her know she is included in his definition of everything. Aubrey blinks repeatedly. Daniel can see the shock mixed with desire in her expression. Daniel enjoys getting the reaction he wants from her. With a smile, he uses his pen to underline his top goal. "Getting invited to the NFL combine is my biggest priority."

Taking his pen from his hand, Aubrey scoots closer, keeping up the intimate tension between the two. Daniel doesn't move. He simply leans back on his forearms, letting her have her way. She's so close she can feel his breath on her shoulder. It raises the hairs on the back of her neck, satisfyingly tickling her. Aubrey realizes she is in a game, playing the position of novice against an expert. She permits a few more seconds to enjoy the moment before taking his book and scooting away.

Chapter Seven

"WHEN IS THE combine?" Aubrey asks.

"The end of March."

Aubrey writes March at the top of the paper. "That means we have six months, which is perfect." She begins making a list starting with month one and ending with month six. "What do you need to accomplish to get an invite?"

"I need to run a fast forty, like exceptionally fast. An exceptional forty will lead me to Grant Lennox, my dream agent. If I get Grant, I know I'll get my invite," he states. "I must be perfect since I'm not playing football. Agents are already skeptical about me, so I need to make them forget."

"Why not just be honest and tell them?"

"Because my shortcomings aren't their business," Daniel answers firmly.

Aubrey studies his eyes only for a short moment before deciding that she isn't going to exhaust herself trying to figure him out. "Alright," she replies effortlessly and then writes the goal at the top of the paper. "You're going to get invited to the combine," Aubrey says matter-of-factly. "You were the cream of the crop in football last year, and this year you will be the cream of the crop in track. We'll record your races, post them on social media, and create heat for you. It will be too much of a good story for sports reporters to resist. The sports world will be talking about you; before you know it, you'll have your invite."

Daniel radiates with joy simply because she believes in him. She is the first person to assure him he will get an invite. His family had politely encouraged him to finish his engineering degree, which was their unspoken way of telling him that he had ruined his chances of making it to the NFL. "You think so?"

"Definitely! You are Daniel Sane. Nothing is impossible for you. You are in control of your destiny," she says, reminding him of his identity.

Daniel's shoulders sit back, and his chest pops forward. "You're right," he says, coming into agreement with her. "And once I get my invite, I'll do amazing and be a first-round pick," he adds to the vision.

Aubrey eagerly writes what he is saying. Daniel keeps his eyes on her as she writes, wanting to understand what it is about her that gives him such pleasure while in her company.

As Aubrey feels his gaze on her, her cheeks warm. "What else?" she asks, hoping to distract him.

Daniel takes the pen and book, adding more goals to the list. They spend the next hour creating a six-month plan to get Daniel's forty-yard-dash time down, national recognition for his speed, and an invite to the NFL combine.

Once they finish the plan, they are zealous about getting started. They get to work immediately. "We're starting with abs because a strong core enables the rest of the body to do what it needs to do properly."

Daniel lifts his shirt, showing off his six-pack. "Done."

His six-pack doesn't impress Aubrey. "A six-pack doesn't automatically equal a strong core. It's one thing to look strong, but are you actually strong?" Aubrey challenges.

Daniel had spent the past six months in his worst mental and physical condition. He wasn't working out, he wasn't eating correctly, and he wasn't in a healthy mental space. Yet, aware that he can be better, Daniel lies flat on the track, preparing for whatever ab workout Aubrey will assign him.

Aubrey stretches out next to him, joining him as he trains. "One hundred bicycles. Let's go." Aubrey counts off their progress as they bring their right elbow to meet their left knee. They do the same with the opposite side of their body. Once they get to number forty, Daniel feels his abdominal muscles stinging. He keeps going as Aubrey is effortlessly flying through them, putting him to shame. Daniel collapses when they reach number sixty, his arms and legs spread wide on the track. "It burns," he complains.

"Push through and give me ten more," Aubrey encourages. "Your body can handle it."

Not wanting to seem weak, Daniel gets back into position and struggles through ten more bicycle crunches. When he finishes, he rolls over and curls into a ball, coddling himself. Aubrey knows he will be successful if he enjoys training and does not see it as a chore, so she takes it easy on him. "I'll give you a five-minute break before we get back into it."

Daniel answers with a groan.

Daniel continues to struggle with completing the exercises when the break is over. Eventually, he grows frustrated. "I'm out of shape, Aubrey," he tells her in a rough tone. "I haven't worked out in six months. I need to build up to where you are. So give me a break."

Aubrey wants to roll her eyes; she is going easy, but she contains herself. "I understand," she replies patiently. "We'll move on to something simpler; it will be the last thing we do today. Since you run with your arms stiff and your fist balled up, we must fix your form. When your form is good, your time should drop automatically." She wiggles her arms and hands as if they are noodles. "When you run, you should be relaxed."

Daniel mimics her movement, wiggling his arms and hands. "No more stiff arms and balled-up fists," he repeats.

Aubrey nods in approval. She put her hands in the proper position—open and relaxed—and pumps her arms slowly. Again, Daniel copies her movements. "That's perfect," Aubrey praises. "Now, keep doing that while walking a mile around the track."

Daniel starts around the track, intentionally keeping his hands and arms relaxed while pumping his arms. After completing a half mile, Daniel stops. "I'm pretty sure I got it," he tells Aubrey. He is stretching his arms and moaning, making it clear that his arms hurt.

Aubrey crosses her arms and pops her hip, growing annoyed because she gave him such an easy task, but he doesn't want to complete it. "We can be done today, but tomorrow there will be no more cheating the process. I need you to finish the workout, or else our plan isn't going to work." Aubrey picks up the plan book and hands it to Daniel. He reads the goal written boldly at the top: Get Invited to the NFL Combine. Run a 4.2 second forty. Be a first-round pick. "Either you want it or not," Aubrey says in a stricter tone before walking toward the exit.

OVER THE NEXT couple of months, Daniel and Aubrey diligently work through Daniel's plan. Aubrey encourages him to stay the course when he wants to skip steps, and Daniel pushes through until he eventually finds his groove. He is stronger and begins finishing Aubrey's workout with ease.

They spend extended time together after training hours. They grab dinner and eat together. They attend the mental success group and spend hours discussing their curriculum.

Aubrey no longer cares if people see them together. Instead, she becomes his daily lunch date in the student union, not wanting one second without him. "You guys have been together a lot lately," Lily comments, inviting herself to join them at the table. "Is this thing finally official yet, or what?"

Aubrey twists her face, shooting her a look of disbelief. "We're officially friends. What about you and Travis? Do y'all have a friendship, or are y'all just high on the physical attraction?" Aubrey asks.

Right on cue, Travis walks over and sits next to Lily. He whispers something in her ear, making Lily giggle in a high pitch. When Travis realizes Daniel and

Aubrey are staring at him, he straightens up. "Did y'all get my flyer?" He holds up his phone, showing the screen. "I'm planning the next big campus event. It's going to be a fashion show and spoken word night all in one," he announces proudly. "I'm recruiting models and poets." Travis looks at Aubrey with a hopeful expression, wanting her to be one of his recruits. "You can model sportswear or whatever else you're comfortable in," Travis throws out in persuasion.

Aubrey stands from the table, gathering her trash. "I'm not a model nor a poet, so count me out. I'll be there to support, though," she tells him. "I must get to class. See you guys at practice later." She glances at Daniel with tenderness before retreating. Daniel watches her walk away as if counting the minutes until they meet again.

"That girl needs to loosen up," Travis chastises behind her back.

Lily gives him a stern look. "It would be nice if you didn't always have something negative to say about my best friend." Travis ignores her complaint, confident in his assessment. "Besides, Daniel can handle that."

"What does she like to do for fun," Daniel inquires.

Lily perks up. "Why? Are you planning to take her out?"

"If she lets me."

"Don't ask her," Lily suggests. "Just surprise her. She absolutely loves rollerblading. We used to rollerblade all day long when we were children."

THE NEXT WEEKEND as Daniel is driving them home from practice, he makes a detour, stopping at a nearby skating rink. When the car stops, Aubrey glances around at their surroundings, then at Daniel, confused.

"I have a surprise for you," he says, reaching into the back seat and pulling out a gift bag. "This is my way of thanking you for helping me."

Aubrey doesn't enjoy surprises. They make her feel out of control. Reluctantly, she accepts the gift, slowly reaching into the bag and pulling out a pair of white rollerblades. Her eyes grow wide as excitement pulses through her, but it quickly fades. Her throat begins to clog, and she is in a battle with tears. Suppressed memories of her childhood flood her thoughts. A vivid memory of her mother smiling beautifully while watching her rollerblade up the driveway makes her heart tighten. Shoving the rollerblades and the memory back into the bag, Aubrey returns the gift to Daniel. Remembering how good life used to be only reminded her of what she's missing currently. "I don't do childish stuff anymore."

"There's nothing wrong with spending a few hours being a kid," Daniel tells her.

"I don't want them," she says, her voice shaky.

The emotion on Aubrey's face is apparent. He decides that she is implacable. Daniel doesn't allow her rejection to affect him. He simply puts the rollerblades in his back seat, saving them for a better time. From the corner of his eye, Daniel sees Aubrey swipe away a tear. He wants to comfort her and ask her what she's feeling, but he let her down the last time she opened up and doesn't feel worthy. They sit quietly in the car, awkwardly looking at the skating rink entrance. A different family exits with their children marveling over arcade prizes every few minutes. Daniel opens his door and leaves his car.

"What are you doing?" Aubrey questions.

"We don't have to skate, but we're going to splurge on some tokens," he says, determined to get Aubrey to have fun. When Aubrey doesn't move, he pokes out his full bottom lip, pleading with her. The corners of her mouth slowly rise, finding Daniel's pleading face adorable and irresistible. Huffing out a sigh of surrender, Aubrey unbuckles her seatbelt and exits the car.

Inside the arcade, Daniel buys a ridiculous number of tokens. He inserts four gold coins into the skee ball slot, sending the balls rushing toward them. Aubrey's competitive nature takes over. She grabs a ball and sends it flying up the lane. In an instant, the two of them transform into children, laughing loudly and overly focused on victory. The game ends with Aubrey winning by just a few points. She throws her hands above her head and swivels her hips. The excitement of beating Daniel makes her miss how he admires her victory dance. His eyes examine her, wondering if she knows how tantalizing and stunning she is. He has a feeling that she is utterly unaware of her perfection.

"Let's play air hockey," she suggests, rushing over to the table before Daniel can respond. Daniel follows her and gets the game going. They go back and forth aggressively until the puck flies across the arcade. Aubrey howls out a melodic and infectious laugh. It is the first time Daniel sees her completely uninhibited. Observing the carefree Aubrey becomes addicting. Every chance he gets, he absorbs her—the way her nose crinkles when she smiles, the joyful sound of her laugh, the movement of her hips when she dances, the sweet scent of her hair when she brushes past him.

They pause their games to refuel. A staff member delivers a barbeque chicken pizza and two smoothies to their table. Aubrey puts her straw into the drink and sips. She moans in approval. "What kind did you get?" He needs to know what she likes.

"Pineapple mango," she answers, sliding her drink in his direction. "You want to try it?"

Daniel doesn't like pineapples, but he wants to taste her, so he wraps her straw with his lips and takes a sip. "Delicious," he raves, not talking about the smoothie. Daniel returns the drink and watches as she comfortably puts her mouth where his lips had just been. He tries not to overthink it, but his mind runs wild with possibilities.

Later that night, when he gets into bed, it feels like she is still with him. He can still hear her laugh in his ear and smell the scent of her hair. When he closes his eyes, he can still see her dancing, but this time she allows him to touch her, so he grabs her hips and dances with her. Her body is soft and molds perfectly into his hands. He pulls her closer to him. She rests her cheek on his shoulder. The taste of her straw lingers in his mouth. He focuses on it until it becomes so palpable that his body reacts to the memory. When he starts imagining more, his eyes fly open, and he sits up in bed, running his hand over his face. "What is happening?" he whispers to himself.

Chapter Eight

AUBREY STRUTS ACROSS CAMPUS with her face toward the sun and peace in her spirit. She skips up the campus library steps and into her mental success group. Daniel is seated in his beanbag when she walks in, staring at the door as if waiting for her. Aubrey notices that he looks at her differently. His demeanor seems more tender than before, making her feel secure in his presence. She eagerly takes the open seat next to him.

"Hey." She delivers the greeting affectionately.

"Hi." Daniel's deep tone seeps like a cool breeze from his lips.

"Yesterday was so much fun. I can't remember the last time I laughed so hard, so thank you."

"Anytime, Aubrey," Daniel replies, his stare pure and gentle.

Drowning in his melanin majesty, Aubrey opens her mouth to comment about the weather just to continue the conversation, but words evade her. The silence between them is electrifying. Daniel's gaze leisurely travels down Aubrey's face, carefully examining every feature—the perfectly arched brows, the shape of her nose, and every beauty mark on her face. When he gets to the curve of her lips, he looks away. He closes his eyes and shakes his head as if his thoughts afflict him. Finally, Daniel releasing his gaze relieves Aubrey. She rubs her hands over the goosebumps on her arms, self-conscious because her body is physically reacting to him.

Thankfully, Adam enters the room, completely distracting Daniel and Aubrey by wearing a blue mask and holding a big box. Daniel and Aubrey turn toward each other with similar peculiar expressions, questioning Adam's sanity.

"No, I haven't completely lost it; I'm just in character. Who knows who I am?" Adam asks the group while setting his box in the middle of the circle.

"The dude from the movie *Avatar*," someone answers.

"You are correct," Adam confirms. "Who can tell me what that movie is about?"

Daniel lifts his arm, and Adam points to him. "A guy puts on a genetically modified body to exist in an atmosphere that would have otherwise been poisonous."

Adam rips off his mask and throws it across the room. "Yes!" he cheers enthusiastically. "He put on something fake to exist in an atmosphere that wasn't for him. That is exactly what we're talking about today. We must kill off our avatars—the fake versions of ourselves that we created to survive in this world—so we can return to being who we were created to be. It happens all the time." Adam opens a box, pulling out a smiley baby doll. "As children, we are vibrant, confident, and believe anything is possible, and then something happens. Maybe it's a tragic event, someone breaks our trust, or someone makes fun of us." Adam takes a living turtle from his box, making everyone gasp as it wiggles its legs. "We go into a shell." He sits the turtle back in the box to pull out a ball cap and sunglasses, putting them on. "Or we hide to protect ourselves until we're unrecognizable. Before we know it, we settle to become a mediocre version of ourselves. Society quenches our power within. Everyone is sick, poor, sad, and oppressed. Where are the prosperous people?" he asks rhetorically. "My appeal to you today is to look within and ask yourself, did something strip away my power? Did I let this world alter my authenticity? You can only become a true culture changer if you're operating in the fullness of the powerful being you were created to be." The entire group sits silently as Adam's words sink in. Adam watches as everyone inwardly analyzes their lives. After a few minutes, he chimes in with an assignment. "You guys have homework. I want you to visit Growth Gardens. Use this piece of paper as your guide." Adam gives everyone a worksheet before dismissing the group.

"Growth Gardens?" Daniel asks as they walk out of class.

Aubrey's eyes grow wide in shock because he hadn't heard about it. "It's a legendary garden on the CSU campus. Mentors usually instruct the students to visit. They like to use creation to deliver a lesson."

"Hmm," Daniel ponders aloud. "Have you been?"

"Of course. It's legendary."

"Let's go learn from creation," Daniel suggests.

"Let's go," Aubrey agrees readily.

They cross the campus and end up at a large wrought iron gate. Daniel pushes through the gate, revealing a marvelous garden stretching across a mile of land. Daniel stands unmoving for a moment, taking it in. Every inch of it is organized and well-kept. The sight of the land makes him feel like he is looking at a picture from a home and garden magazine. The raised garden beds are made of polished wood labeled with chic black and white signage to differentiate the vegetables from the fruit and the flowers from the herbs. Daniel and Aubrey explore the garden, walking along a crisp gray concrete path. They pass a garden bed labeled strawberries, a bed labeled caneberries, and a garden of cabbage. A line of fruit trees behind the garden beds closes out the garden. Each tree has a pear, plum, peach, or apple label.

"Find the garden bed of rescue plants." Daniel reads their assignment from the piece of paper as they walk.

Aubrey points to a black-and-white tin sign that reads *Rescue Plants*. They stop in front of the garden bed, looking at the plants that are little sprouts in their seedling pots. "These rescue plants are in danger of mediocrity," Aubrey reads the assignment. "They need to be grounded in an environment where they can thrive and reach their full potential. So choose a plant and find a garden bed for it for it to thrive in."

"Which plant do you want to pick?" Daniel asks when she finishes reading.

"Let's think about this." Aubrey crosses her arms and takes her time eyeing the choices before her.

Daniel watches her; she scrunches her nose while pondering. She cants her head, in deep concentration, for minutes without any sign of coming out.

"Commitment issues?"

Breaking away from her thoughts, she smirks while playfully cutting her eyes as she chooses a plant marked as a sunflower though it doesn't look like much. "I'm thinking this, but let's research first."

"Of course. Can't commit without the research," Daniel remarks, the irony spilling from his tone.

Ignoring him, Aubrey pulls out her phone and researches sunflower needs. Feeling confident they can get the sunflower to reach its full potential, she returns her phone to her pocket. "This is the one," she confirms.

Daniel and Aubrey find a garden bed with enough room for the sunflower to thrive and plant it. "A drip irrigation system will keep your plant watered," Daniel reads the final instruction. "Come back as often as necessary to watch your plant flourish."

LATER THAT DAY, at track practice, Coach set up mini hurdles for the team to practice speed drills. "Aubrey, can you please show everyone how it's done?" Coach asks.

Aubrey walks up to the miniature hurdles and runs over them as if they aren't there.

"Beautiful!" Coach praises Aubrey for executing the drill effortlessly. "That's how it's done. You get the most power when you bring your heel over your knee." Coach stands on one leg while lifting his other leg high enough for his heel to rise above his knee, demonstrating once again. "If you do that, speed will propel you down the track. So line up, and let's get it done. I don't want to see anyone kicking over my hurdles," Coach warns.

Travis is first in line. He completes the mini hurdles expertly. Lily and Jade each kick over one hurdle, frustrating Coach. "Pick up your feet. Heel over knee," he reminds them. When it's Daniel's turn, he chops through the drill like a football player, knocking over several hurdles. Coach groans. "That would have been great if you were on the turf, but this is a track. Try it again, but try sprinting through, don't chop," Coach instructs.

Daniel puts the hurdles back in place and tries again. This time he doesn't chop his feet; he runs through the drill, causing him to knock over more hurdles. Coach simply runs his hand over his face while mumbling something. Daniel can see Coach's reserved frustration and lets it get to him. He continues knocking over the hurdles during each repetition of the drill.

"Again," Coach challenges Daniel, picking up the hurdles and putting them back in place. Daniel tries again with the same outcome. Every time Coach must reposition one of the mini hurdles, he groans.

Letting out a sigh through his teeth, Coach turns away from Daniel. "You can stop trying."

Daniel stomps away from the team, and Aubrey follows him.

"I can show you how to—" Aubrey begins.

"Did I ask for your help?" Daniel snaps, cutting her sentence short.

Aubrey's head pulls back, and she crosses her arms, taken aback by his attitude. Aubrey turns to walk away, but something inside her won't let her keep silent. "You know what your problem is? You care too much about what other people think of you. That's why you hide your faults. You're so busy creating this perfect public perception that you won't even allow yourself to go through the process. Maybe that's your avatar—the infallible one. Mr. Can't-do-wrong."

"And your avatar is self-preservation," Daniel fires back. "You will do anything to preserve your feelings, even if it keeps you from connecting with others. You only have one friend. You won't let anyone else get close to you because you're still holding on to that lifeless situation with your mom. Let it go. Maybe then you can be emotionally available and show up in this world as the person you were created to be." As he walks away, Aubrey knows how he truly feels about her. It hurt to hear the words out loud, but she already knew that about herself deep down. Perhaps, Daniel knew she was right about him, too; that's why he slapped her back with the truth.

When practice is over, Aubrey goes into the rehab room to take an ice bath to recover her muscles and feelings. After thirty minutes alone, she feels calm. She walks out of the rehab room into an almost empty arena. Daniel is lying on his back, blankly looking up at the ceiling. The mini hurdles are next to him, sprawled every which way from being knocked over. Rolling her eyes and shaking her head, Aubrey starts toward the exit. With each step she takes, she feels her legs get heavier as if her body is trying to communicate that she's heading in the wrong direction. Finally, when reaching the exit and putting one foot in front of the other feels impossible, she turns and walks in his direction. She approaches him and kneels in front of his head. Daniel looks up at her, happy to see her vibrant face above his.

"I apologize for how I spoke to you earlier. I

shouldn't have said it," Daniel speaks softly.

Aubrey lifts her shoulders and lets them drop carefreely. "It was the truth."

"What you said about me is somewhat true too."

Aubrey giggles. "Somewhat?"

Daniel releases a breath. "I do care what people think. I want to get this stuff so badly and prove to everyone that I'm not a failure," he admits in a low tone.

"That's the wrong reason. You don't have to prove anything to anyone. Do it for yourself and do it to change the culture. How will you use your influence when you make it to the NFL?" Aubrey asks.

He takes a moment to think. "I want to urge people to stop giving their past so much authority over their future. Instead, let dead situations die and find life by constantly pursuing new opportunities," Daniel says passionately.

Aubrey crosses her arms. "Are you talking about yourself or me?"

Daniel pushes himself up to a standing position and starts putting the mini hurdles in the proper place. "I'm talking about us and anyone else struggling to see their future because they're still living in the past."

Aubrey also stands, commanding his attention. "I'm not giving my past authority. I'm seeking ways to have a future with my mom," Aubrey corrects him before stepping toward the door.

"I would love your help," Daniel calls out humbly.

Aubrey pivots, turning back toward him. His eyes are genuinely vulnerable, communicating that he needs her. Aubrey's irritation ceases almost immediately. "Sure," she agrees. She wonders if he knows he is the only person who can penetrate her barrier with a look.

"I appreciate you so much."

Aubrey ignores his sentiment to focus on handling business. She slowly walks through the hurdles, showing Daniel how his heel should come over his knee. Daniel does what she says, sauntering through the drill. He doesn't knock over any hurdles. "That was perfect. Now do the same thing using your speed."

Daniel does the same thing but sprints instead of walking. When he is finished, he eagerly looks over his shoulder to see if the hurdles are still standing. They are. He throws his arms above his head and gazes toward the ceiling. He stands like that for a long moment. Eventually, he looks for Aubrey, who is clapping while wearing an angelic smile.

"And that's how you combine your speed with perfect form. Do that at the track meet this weekend, and they might be saying your name on SportsCenter again. *Former football star Daniel Sane is making a name for himself in the world of track and field. That man is fast, and his form is perfect,*" Aubrey states, imitating the voice of a sportscaster.

Daniel howls out a loud laugh.

DANIEL'S CONFIDENCE IS HIGH as he gets ready for his first race as a track athlete. He warms up alongside Aubrey, Travis, Lily, and Jade. They are all running the sixty-meter dash. Each has earbuds, listening to music that mentally prepares them to run their best race. The closer they get to the start of the race, the more spaced-out Daniel seems to be. Aubrey eyes him, figuring that he is in the zone. She doesn't bother him. But, as the official calls the men to the track, Daniel looks at her and lets out a nervous breath.

"You're ready. Your form is perfect. All you have to do is add the Daniel Sane speed to it," she whispers.

He responds with an encouraged smile.

Daniel and Travis walk on the track, setting up their starting blocks. They strip off their warmup clothes and stand in front of the blocks, waiting for the umpire to start the race.

"Mmmm," Jade hums aloud, falling into a trance as her eyes travel over Daniel in his fitted uniform. Aubrey and Lily turn toward Jade with their mouths hanging open, shocked by her blatant thirst. "Are y'all dating?" Jade asks audaciously, never taking her eyes away from Daniel.

"We're friends," Aubrey answers undecidedly, feeling the need to stamp a claim on him.

A lustful beam lights up Jade's face. Aubrey follows Jade's line of sight to Daniel standing on the track and instantly understands where Jade is coming from. His physique, enhanced by the small uniform, is awfully distracting. She commands her thoughts to focus on the race that is beginning.

"Runners, take your marks," the umpire announces. Daniel, Travis, and runners from the opposing teams get down into their starting blocks. The entire arena is silent as the umpire's hand goes up. "Get set." Aubrey's heart stops beating as she anticipates the sound of the gun. She wants Daniel to win more than she wants herself to win. She wants his first race to be the beginning of him regaining his confidence and the sports world's attention.

The gun goes off with a loud bang. The guys explode from their blocks, running as fast as they can.

Aubrey cheers Daniel's name loudly until he crosses the finish line. Aubrey looks at the instant replay screen, seeing Daniel's name and time appear first. Daniel won. Aubrey takes off toward the finish line to congratulate him. In an instant, Jade appears, wrapping her arms and legs around him just as she is about to leap into his arms. Coach is there, too, along with the rest of the team. Everyone gathers around Daniel, making a seismic fuss about his win. Aubrey finds herself being just another face in the crowd. By the time she gets to him, the excitement has dwindled. She extends her arm to fist bump while Daniel extends his arms to hug her, which creates an awkward moment of them trying to figure out if they should embrace or fist bump. Finally, they settle on a fist bump. "Great job!" Aubrey sings excitedly. "That was amazing!"

"Thank you," he says with intense eyes, wanting her to know that he is thanking her for everything she has done for him.

"Anytime," she replies, her eyes just as intense.

Daniel and Aubrey sport gold medals around their necks when the meet ends. Lily looks back and forth between them with a proud expression. "I need a photo of this," she says. "Daniel, stand next to Aubrey," Lily instructs. Daniel and Aubrey stand beside each other with a foot of space between them. Lily gestures with her hands for them to move closer together. They take a small step toward each other until they are just inches from touching. Aubrey can feel the heat radiating from his skin, inviting her in. Instead, she inches away. Knowing her, Lily simply snaps the photo without bringing attention to Aubrey's aversion to connection.

"We gotta celebrate, bro," Travis proposes. "Get together at my place. I'll invite the team."

"How about an intimate gathering, just us four at my place," Daniel suggests.

Travis' shoulders slump, but he goes along with the plans.

LATER THAT EVENING, the four of them gather around Daniel's small kitchen island as he sets out take-out food and soft drinks that he picked up from the grocery store. "This is for you," Daniel says, pulling one last item from the grocery bag and handing it to Aubrey.

She stares at the package of Airheads candies in his hand without taking them. The shock and confusion are apparent on her face. Finally, she turns her attention to Lily. "You told him about this too?"

"I did not," Lily informs innocently. "I only told him about the rollerblades."

Aubrey turns back to Daniel, still with his arm extended, waiting for her to take the candy. "She didn't tell me anything," Daniel assures Aubrey. "Why? What did I miss?"

"What made you buy this for me?" she questions.

Daniel shrugs. "I saw the candy in the aisle, and your face popped into my head. So I just listened to the inkling."

Reaching out, Aubrey finally takes the candy from him, handling it like a precious stone. "I used to eat these all the time as a child. My mom used to bring them home from the store whenever she went grocery shopping," she explains in a small voice.

The moment becomes static and thoughtful. "Oh," Daniel breathes.

"Right," she replies in the same quiet tone while staring at the candy.

Lily, Travis, and Daniel watch her, noticing how she diligently holds back tears. They all know Aubrey would prefer they ignore her than console her, so Daniel deflects. "We might as well eat and then play the game Trav brought."

They start making their plates. Daniel slides a plate of food in front of Aubrey. Everyone sits around her, making small talk. As they eat, Aubrey slowly emerges from her trance, picking up her fork and joining the lighthearted conversation. She laughs at their jokes and even adds some humor of her own. By the time they start playing Taboo, she feels like herself again. "Alright, Daniel. You ready?" Aubrey asks, preparing to compete against Lily and Travis.

"Ready!" Daniel rubs his hands together, anticipating the win.

Lily stands over Aubrey's shoulder, watching her with hawk eyes so she can buzz her if she says the Taboo words. "Here we go," Aubrey starts the game. "Middle. You got over the…" Aubrey gives a clue.

"Hump. Wednesday," Daniel answers.

"Yup," Aubrey confirms and moves on to the next. "Person, mulch, tulip."

"Gardner," Daniel guesses.

"Mm hmm," she praises.

"Between five a.m. and six a.m. God."

"The sunrise," Daniel answers.

"That's right!"

They went on to score ten points in a row. The timer goes off, and they high-five in celebration.

"Don't get too excited," Travis contests, getting in position for his turn.

Lily calls out the first clue. "In a pattern on the floor."

"Carpet," Travis guesses.

"No. In a pattern outside," Lily tries again. "It's not blue, but?"

"Pink?" Travis guesses.

"No!" Lily groans, growing frustrated. "Outside, in a pattern," she delivers the clue more harshly.

"In a pattern outside?" Trav repeats slowly, thinking over the clue, and the timer goes off.

"It was bricks!" Lily yells, tossing the game aside.

"Bricks aren't blue," Travis complains. "Why would you say blue?"

"I couldn't say red, so I tried to get you to guess." She grinds her teeth together, then turns her frustration toward Aubrey and Daniel. "You guys had to be cheating," Lily accuses. "There's no way you guys got every one of those right."

"That's what I'm saying," Travis jumps in to agree with Lily.

"How did we cheat?" Daniel asks with a chuckle. "You brought this game, and we never even played before. Aubrey and I are just tapped into each other."

Aubrey and Daniel's eyes meet from across the room, gazing at each other with encompassing softness. Both are aware of Travis and Lily's presence, but they don't allow any distractions. Lily takes Travis' hand, carefully pulling him toward the door so they can escape, giving Aubrey and Daniel privacy. The sound of the door closing brings Daniel and Aubrey out of their reverie. "I should go too," Aubrey murmurs, standing.

"Why?"

"To rest."

"Can I please have one more hour of your time?" he solicits. "I just want to sit in your company."

Aubrey gradually lowers back to her seat on his sofa, bringing her knees to her chest, allowing him to dive into her eyes. Daniel's breathing is even, and his eyes are low as he peers at her. "Can I ask you something?" she says. "What about me intrigues you? I mean, I'm emotionally unavailable, right?"

"Nah." Daniel shakes his head, retracting what he once said about her. "You're just looking for a soft place to land. You'll open up everything once I show you I'm a safe space for you. I want you completely uninhibited like that day at the skating rink. You danced, you laughed, and the pain didn't confine you. That girl intrigues me. I want her every day."

Aubrey feels her heart pound in a slow yet violent thud. Every beat is unhurried but impacts her entire being. She wonders if he knows how much she needs him, that the soft place is crucial to her survival.

Chapter Nine

THE NEXT DAY, Daniel and Aubrey walk into track practice together, their steps in sync as they approach Travis and Lily. As Aubrey joins their warmup, stretching her hamstrings, she feels Lily's eyes on her. Lily is wearing a smirk on her face. At first, Aubrey pretends not to see her because she knows what Lily is thinking. Lily had creeped out of Daniel's apartment the night before so Aubrey and Daniel could have alone time. But, of course, Lily wants details.

"Nothing happened. We just sat and talked," Aubrey reports dryly as if Lily should know her by now.

"Oh, I know," Lily states confidently, letting Aubrey know that she indeed does know her.

"So, why are you looking at me like that?" she asks, annoyed by Lily's smirk.

"What do you love most about him?"

Aubrey twists her lips and narrows her eyes. "What are you doing?"

"You love him."

"He is my friend. I enjoy him," she modifies.

"There is something about him that has you glowing."

Aubrey shrugs. "He inspires me to be my highest self, and I love that."

"You love him?" Lily questions enthusiastically.

"I *love* that he inspires me."

Lily rolls her eyes. "Well, you remind me of someone I haven't seen in about five or so years. Her name is Aubrey Blake."

Aubrey stops stretching, giving Lily her full attention. "I remind you of myself?" Aubrey asks, wanting clarity.

"The real you. Not the shell of a woman walking around here pretending to be you. Your skin is glowing. Your smile is real. I can see the life coming back."

Aubrey's eyes drift upward as she takes a moment to understand Lily's statement. Lily has known Aubrey since she was a bubbly child. She saw the transition from the true Aubrey to the avatar Aubrey. She recognizes that Aubrey is shedding the fake version of herself she created to survive in the world. Aubrey becomes proud of herself for learning to release. She also realizes that Lily has been dealing with her behavior while remaining a loyal friend.

Coach blows his whistle, and the team stands up to meet him across the track. Aubrey falls into step with Lily as the group walks over, playfully bumping her with her hip. She laces her arm through Lily's arm. "Thank you, Lil, for being a friend, sister, and my person in this crazy world."

"No need to thank me. However, as my first successful client, you can write a testimonial to vouch for my services." They laugh while walking arm in arm over to Coach.

"You guys have been diligently working the last few weeks, so we're going to have some fun today," Coach announces when the team reaches him. "Today's practice will be a circuit race. We'll split into two teams. The winning team will get to have tomorrow off." Coach points to Daniel then Aubrey. "You two are my team captains because you won all your races at yesterday's track meet. Come on up. Aubrey, you have the first pick."

Narrowing her gaze, she scans the team, focused on winning a day off track practice. "I pick Travis." Her choice is purely strategic. Travis is the best choice to keep up with Daniel.

"I got Jade," Daniel counters. His pick is smart since Jade is the second-fastest girl on the team. It irritates Aubrey to see Jade bounce into Daniel's arms, hanging onto him. Aubrey looks away, attempting to convince herself that she doesn't care even though she does.

Aubrey's next choice is simple. "Lily," she picks.

Daniel goes on to pick the next fastest guy on the team. They choose back and forth until everyone has a team. Once the teams are together, Coach explains each circuit workout and blows his whistle, starting the game. Daniel and Travis weave through a set of cones, chopping their feet to help navigate the course. Aubrey cheers for Travis even though she finds pleasure in watching Daniel speed through the cones ahead of Travis. The next part of the circuit is low jumps, and Travis catches up to Daniel. His slender build gives him a slight advantage. Next, they must run through mini hurdles without knocking any over. Travis and

Daniel complete that part of the race perfectly, but Travis is still ahead. The last part of the race is to complete fifty burpees. Again, Daniel moves with skill and agility, catching up to Travis. The race is even when Daniel and Travis get to the handoff zone. Travis taps Aubrey's hand, and she takes off, low-walking through the next part of the course. Jade is close behind her, but Aubrey keeps her attention on the race she's running. She feels an intense tightening in her calf muscle near the end of the low-walking section. The pain is sudden and crippling. She howls out an ear-bleeding scream while rolling over to her back and grabbing her leg. Coach and Daniel rush over to her. Coach bends down and reaches out, but Aubrey flinches away from him, causing Coach to pull his hands away quickly.

"Where does it hurt?" Coach asks.

"A cramp in my calf," she breathes. "Just need a minute."

Two minutes pass, and Aubrey is still rolling around, trying to soothe the cramp. Her screams are getting more severe. "Where is the trainer?" Coach calls across the arena.

"She's not in there," one of Aubrey's teammates informs.

Daniel bends down next to Aubrey to whisper in her ear. "You need help. So, I'm going to pick you up and carry you to the rehab room, alright?"

Helplessly nodding, Aubrey grants him permission to carry her. Daniel slowly scoops Aubrey into his arms. She buries her face between his shoulder and his neck, breathing heavily. Daniel moves quickly to get her in the rehab room, placing her on one of the tables. He scans the offices, looking for a trainer, but every office is empty. "The training staff must be in a meeting or something," he says once he's back to Aubrey. "If you'd let me, I can massage out the cramp."

Aubrey nods, wanting the pain to go away, and Daniel begins massaging gently over her aching muscle. He is careful and thoughtful with her body, moving purposefully over her calf muscle only. Within seconds, the pain subsides, and a different ache begins to release. Daniel's tender touch confronts her with serenity and consolation. Just like those who claim to see and hear everything, Aubrey feels everything. She can feel every bit of Daniel's affection releasing into her. It floods her like a raging sea. She is saturated with his sentiment. The thickness in her throat comes on strong as she experiences how his hands console her body and melts her heart. Closing her eyes, Aubrey tries to block the emotion from escaping, but the tears start flowing from the side of her eyes, dropping in blobs on the table. Daniel stops moving his hands. "You okay?" he asks, worried that he may have done something wrong.

Aubrey gives up on trying to save face and allows herself to release. She sits on the table and wraps her arms around Daniel's neck, bringing their bodies together for the first time. Aubrey hugs him tightly, breathing in his scent and warming herself on his skin. Daniel embraces her, rubbing his hands up and down her back. The moment completely overtakes Aubrey. She indulges in the feeling of being sheltered and cherished by someone who genuinely cares. It feels like someone removed a barrier, allowing her to run freely in an open field. The tears elevate to sobs. Daniel doesn't react. He simply squeezes her tighter, knowing what she needs. They hold on to each other for twenty minutes before Aubrey releases the hold around his neck. When she pulls away, she runs her hands over her red and puffy face, releasing a sigh.

"Thank you," she breathes.

Daniel replies with a warm, gentle kiss on her forehead.

After experiencing Daniel's touch, Aubrey can't get enough. Simply being cheek-to-cheek with him gives her a recharge that she wasn't aware she needed. Upon greeting him, she jumps into his arms, reveling in how his solid arms feel around her body. His lips inadvertently brush against her neck as he pulls her close. Aubrey enjoys it. Whenever she is in his presence, she rests her cheek on his arm to feel the heat radiate from his body. And when it is time to depart at night, she holds on to him for minutes, not wanting the moment to end.

One evening as Daniel and Aubrey sit on the couch studying, Aubrey leans her head on Daniel's shoulder as usual. Daniel leans in to kiss her on the cheek, but his lips land at the corner of her mouth. It is dangerously close to a kiss. Aubrey glances up at him to see if it is accidental or purposeful. The hungry look in his eyes lets her know that it is intentional. He is trying to see how far she will let him go.

She stands from the couch to put distance between them. She feels it is her fault for hanging all over him. She has given him the wrong idea and will have to fix it. "I'm going to make a smoothie. You want one?" she asks while walking into the kitchenette.

"I'll help." Daniel stands and follows behind her. Opening the freezer, he takes out strawberries and tosses them to the counter. The bag lands with a loud thud. Aubrey observes as he aggressively grabs the bananas and carelessly tosses them next to the strawberries.

"Okay," Aubrey sighs, knowing precisely what frustrated him. "We may as well talk about it."

"How long are we going to do this friend-zone thing?" he huffs.

"The friend zone isn't a negative thing."

Daniel stares at her with tired eyes. He doesn't want to hear anything about being friends anymore.

"I'll explain," Aubrey says when he doesn't respond. She opens the bag of strawberries and puts a few in the blender. Then she adds a banana. "A girl and a guy meet. They have a physical attraction, so they decide to get together." Aubrey presses the pulse button on the blender to mix the strawberries and bananas. She goes into the refrigerator, taking out a pack of raw chicken breast. She pierces the package and pours some chicken juice onto the counter before opening the top of the blender.

Daniel's mouth falls open. "Are you thinking about putting raw chicken juice in my blender?"

"If I did, the smoothie would be contaminated, right?"

Daniel nods impatiently, wanting her to get to her point so he can make his point next.

"Even though the smoothie is contaminated, it will still look good," Aubrey continues. "Most people would eat the smoothie because it looks good. They won't take the time to check to see if it's contaminated. And by the time they know it's contaminated, it's already too late because they ate it already."

Daniel crosses his arms. "Are you trying to say I look good, but I'm contaminated?"

"I just don't know you like that."

"I hate when you say that," Daniel complains. "You said the same thing about your mom, which makes me feel like I'm being punished for her faults."

"I'm saying I don't know you well enough. You have secrets and whatever else going on. That's why we're friends," she tells him.

Daniel rolls his eyes, growing more frustrated with her. "You know me, and you knew it from the first day we met. You're just refusing to admit it."

Aubrey says nothing, knowing that he's right. Their spirits knew each other before they ever met physically. It is difficult to put into words, so she buries it.

"So, are you hugging your other friends like you are hugging all over me?" he continues to challenge her.

Guilt pulses through Aubrey. All the times she has hugged Daniel, it was selfish, and she knew it. She greedily wanted to feel his warmth and touch while maintaining their friendship. She could handle it, but it didn't mean he was strong enough to handle it. Instead of answering his question, she diverts her attention to his phone conveniently flashing across the room. "Your phone is ringing."

Daniel ignores his phone, not letting anything distract him from the conversation. "The answer is no. You don't lay all over anyone like you do on me," he concludes.

"What do you want from me," she asks, exhausted.

"Some intention just as I have intentions for you."

What intentions?" Aubrey ponders aloud.

Daniel points to his Life Plan book and then opens the book. Aubrey sees that he has added a new goal to the list. She sees her name scribbled across the bottom. For some reason, it makes her heart race.

"When I dream about draft day, I imagine you there with my family and me." Daniel slowly wraps her in his arms, hugging her from behind to whisper in her ear. "I think about ending up across the country but being at peace because my family and the only other person I care for deeply will be moving with me. I see us waking up early in the mornings and talking just like we do now. Cooking together in a big kitchen."

His intentions suffocate Aubrey, mainly because she can't envision herself moving across the country with him without knowing everything about him. Words evade her. She stands stiffly in his arms, thinking of something to say.

Daniel waits for her to respond. After a full minute passes and she doesn't respond, he knows that her intentions aren't the same. The muscle in his jaw tightens as he releases his arms around her. He looks away to hide his hurt.

"I don't want to follow my heart. I want to lead my heart the proper way," Aubrey rationalizes.

"Well, lead it toward me! It's not that complicated!"

Aubrey remains quiet, unwilling to talk to him when he becomes irritated.

Realizing this, Daniel speaks in a softer tone. "I just want to know that I have your heart."

"God has my heart," she says with heavy sarcasm.

"Do I at least have a small piece? Does your heart desire me at all?"

Of course, she thinks to herself. She struggles to convey her feelings with adequate words, so she stays quiet.

Daniel snatches up the plan book and turns it to a blank page. He slams a pen on top of the paper. "What do you see in your future? Write it down."

"I don't know what to write."

"Anything you see in your future. Do you see me? Do you see anything at all?"

Aubrey begins writing on the paper. Daniel watches her write. When she is finished, she drops the pen. Daniel reads the one sentence that she wrote. RECONNECT WITH MY MOM.

He isn't part of her plans for the future. Growing even more annoyed with her reluctance to express her feelings, Daniel opens his mouth to ask her to leave, but before he can get out the words, his door opens, and Kennedy comes strolling in. "You're kidding!" Daniel chastises his sister.

Chapter Ten

"I CALLED FIRST, but you don't answer my calls anymore," Kennedy relays, full of mockery. "I thought I'd come to meet the girl who takes up all of my brother's time." Kennedy walks toward Aubrey and extends her hand. "My name is Kennedy. Nice to meet you."

Aubrey politely shakes her hand. "Hi, my name is Aubrey."

"You two spend a lot of time together. Things must be getting pretty seri—" Kennedy begins to pry, but Aubrey's head starts moving from side to side before Kennedy can finish her sentence.

"We're just friends," she informs Kennedy with emphasis.

Kennedy peeks at Daniel from the corner of her eyes before looking back to Aubrey, completely skeptical. "Just friends?" she pries again. "I'm interested to know why? My brother's a quality man, so I know he's good enough for you."

"Let it go, Kennedy," Daniel cautions his sister.

"I just want to know," she continues, not heeding his caution. "And if you're only friends, why spend all his time? What more do you want?"

Picking up on the sassiness in Kennedy's inflection, Aubrey braces herself for confrontation. "I just want to know exactly who I'm getting involved with," Aubrey answers bluntly, not being one to cower. Aubrey turns toward Daniel, ensuring he also knows where she is coming from. "That means the truth about why you aren't playing football."

Kennedy takes a step closer to Aubrey, demanding her eyes.

"Kennedy!" Daniel grabs his sister's arm, but she snatches away.

"That's none of your business, though," Kennedy tells Aubrey.

"If he wants to be in a relationship with me, everything about him is my business," Aubrey rebuts.

"Are you sure you're not after his money? Or trying to get pregnant?"

A humorless giggle escapes Aubrey's lips, laughing at the situation's absurdity. She focuses her attention back on Daniel. "I'm not moving across the country with someone I don't know and who treats me like I'm unreasonable for wanting to know, so let's agree to be done." Aubrey walks past Kennedy and Daniel and out of his apartment, slamming the door behind her.

Kennedy plops down on Daniel's couch, crossing her legs. "Hope you've been practicing self-control."

"You cannot just walk into my apartment!" Daniel roars.

"Well, answer my calls!" Kennedy yells back. A sudden wave of emotion fills her eyes. "I worry about you. I'm the one who found you unconscious."

Daniel blows out a tired sigh and calmly walks over to sit next to his sister. He pulls her into a hug, rubbing her back. "I apologize for making you go through that. I guarantee you that it will never happen again. But I need you to believe me and let me live."

AUBREY STANDS AGAINST the wall, carefully stretching her calf muscle when she spots Daniel approaching from her peripheral view. His face is all business. The friendship is gone. "Hey," he greets in a uniform tone.

"Hey," Aubrey replies, matching his tone.

"Just wanted to apologize for my sister's behavior last night. She was wrong."

"Apology accepted."

"Also, I wanted to be clear and tell you that I will *never* speak about what I did. That man is dead." He pauses, emphasizing his statement. "Dead situations don't deserve life. If you want to continue trying to dig up a dead version of me, that's your choice and your loss. I'm going to continue growing into the best version of myself." Without another word, he turns and walks away.

Aubrey feels void and grief the moment he's gone, knowing she doesn't have her dearest friend to reach out to anymore. But she is proud of herself for sticking to her standards. She leaves the wall with her head high and joins her team as they stretch in a circle. Bending down to touch her toes, Aubrey wonders how she will manage to be in the same place as Daniel without being friendly. She thinks of all the spaces they share and concludes that they need to figure out a way to be cordial. As she mentally constructs a plan, loud giggling breaks her focus. Following the sound of laughter, Aubrey glances over her shoulder. Her gaze lands on Daniel and Jade sitting side by side, leaning into each other, snickering. The two of them together look like a ridiculously attractive couple. Aubrey sucks in a breath that she can't seem to let out. She stands there, not breathing, feeling like someone has knocked the wind out of her.

"What is going on?" Lily demands, tugging on Aubrey's arm, saving her away from gawking at Daniel as he flirts with Jade.

"We decided to end our friendship," Aubrey clarifies indifferently.

"Why?" Lily questions, passionate and perplexed.

"He has secrets. I don't have the patience."

Lily's green eyes cut into her. "So, you're going to let her swoop in and grab your man?"

"If she can grab him, sis can have him." Aubrey turns away, convincing herself that she does not care. But, in reality, seeing Daniel snuggled with Jade is disheartening.

Aubrey spends the rest of practice constantly redirecting her thoughts away from deciding which one she will choke first.

Coach watches as Aubrey powers through the workout like a mad woman. He reminds the team to run at 70 percent. Aubrey runs at 90 percent. Coach tells her to slow down. She runs faster. Crossing his arms, he assesses what is happening. He sees Jade cheesing in Daniel's face and connects the dots. He sighs impatiently. "That's it for today." He dismisses the team early. "Daniel, can I see you for a moment?"

Daniel jogs over and gives Coach his full attention. "What's up, Coach?"

The CSU staff took their mentorship role seriously. They honored their position to influence the students. When Coach Aaron notices a student making faulty decisions, he feels the need to call it out. "What are you doing flip-flopping between these girls?" he probes, transitioning from track coach to life coach.

"I'm not flip-flopping. Aubrey doesn't want me, so I'm moving on."

"Moving on to somebody who's just convenient right now? Do you truly want her?"

Daniel gapes at Coach with his lip hanging. Of course, Jade isn't who he truly wants.

"Listen to me," Coach continues. "If you don't want Jade, don't lead her on. Furthermore, don't play yourself and lose who you truly want. Most importantly, learn to master yourself, and you'll attract good things. You will never have to chase. Let that sink in." Coach claps him on the shoulder and walks away.

THE NEXT FEW WEEKS are brutal for Aubrey and Daniel. They miss each other, but neither is willing to admit it. Every time Aubrey walks by Daniel, his head involuntarily follows. In the student union, Daniel cannot resist peeking at Aubrey even though he is sitting at a table with Jade. Aubrey eats her food while joking with Lily, not seeming pressed about their breakup in the least bit, so Daniel tries not to let it bother him, either. Instead, he focuses on Jade and picks up on the conversation he had been tuning out.

"See," she said, turning her phone screen toward him. "That's my dress." Daniel glances at the model on the screen wearing a short backless red dress. "It arrives tomorrow, just in time for the fashion show. I can't wait to take some cute pics together and post them on the Gram." She sways her shoulders, anticipating a good time. "We're both wearing red, right? They're gonna be jealous!"

"I'm going to be unavailable," he tells her gently.

Jade's green eyes pierce him. "Excuse me! What are you talking about?"

Irritation pulses through him for getting involved with Jade in the first place. He thought Jade would be a beautiful distraction from Aubrey, but after a few conversations, he wasn't too fond of her. The two were on opposite ends of the spectrum regarding morals, values, and beliefs. He tried to be diplomatic about ending things, but she kept appearing like an annoying fly. "I'm unavailable to go to the fashion show with you."

"Every time I ask you to do something, you're unavailable. So just give me the real?"

"I'm feeling someone else, and that's not fair to you. I apologize," Daniel tells her honestly. "They're still gonna be jealous when they see you come through in your red dress."

Jade looks over her shoulder, glaring at Aubrey from head to toe. She looks back at Daniel with the same glare before rolling her eyes and retreating from the table.

Daniel refocuses his attention in Aubrey's direction, seeing her exit the student union. He knows her schedule well enough to know that she is heading home to get some rest before track practice. Gathering his things, Daniel leaves the student union too. Daniel can see Aubrey's car about two hundred meters ahead as he drives home. She turns into their parking lot a few minutes before him. By the time he parks, she is already inside the building. Daniel rushes inside, hoping to catch her on the elevator. Just as the doors are closing, he slides inside. Aubrey looks at him for a split second before looking away as if he is a stranger. Daniel hadn't planned to say anything to Aubrey. He just wanted to be in her vicinity to see how she would react. It isn't the reaction he hoped for. He thought they would do the thing where they gazed into each other's eyes while exchanging a smitten smile. Instead, they stand with their posture turned away from each other in opposite corners of the elevator.

The sound of Aubrey's phone vibrating fills the small space. She pulls her phone from her pocket and checks the screen. The phone buzzes as she stares at Jace's name, contemplating whether to answer or ignore it. Jace has been calling since she ran into him on campus, but she has ignored his calls until she feels ready to talk. Now, she feels prepared to speak to Jace. She needs Daniel to know he isn't the only one who could move on to someone else.

"Hello?"

"You finally answered," Jace says with a brazen confidence.

"Mm hmm," she confirms. "What's up?"

"I'm trying to catch up with you. Can we do that?"

"What did you have in mind?" Aubrey investigates.

Daniel can hear every word Jace is speaking through her phone. He clenches his teeth, growing upset with Aubrey and himself. Daniel had taken the first shot by spending time with Jade. Now that Aubrey is firing back, he feels wounded.

"I was thinking about how good you would look on my arm at the fashion show," Jace invites.

"You're talking about Trav's fashion show, right?" Aubrey knows that Daniel will be there and see them together. A small part of her wants to spare his feelings, but he didn't care about her feelings when walking around with Jade on his arm.

"Yep," Jace tells her.

Clearing his throat loudly, Daniel turns toward Aubrey. He stares at her, intent on relaying his disapproval. She looks up, seeing his entreating look. His eyes are annoyingly effective. Even though she wants to be petty and vindictive, she cares for him too much to put him through the same thing he is putting her through.

Looking away, she waits for the effect to wear off and proceeds, doing what she feels she must do to earn respect. "Yeah, I'll grace your arm," Aubrey accepts Jace's invite. "I'll meet you there."

She ends the call and stands tall, wearing a spiteful smirk.

"You feel good about yourself?" Daniel confronts. "This is that emotional stuff. You're following your heart right now instead of leading it."

The smirk transforms into a booming laugh. Aubrey doubles over while holding her stomach, mocking his feelings. "Your audacity is hilarious!"

The elevator doors open, and Aubrey walks out and into her apartment, still laughing. Daniel stands stiffly for a moment before taking out his phone and pressing a button. "Trav, I need you to do something for me."

_____

ON FASHION SHOW NIGHT, Aubrey takes extra time in the shower, shaving until every inch of her is smooth. She takes her time straightening her hair, letting it fall around her shoulders like silk. She puts on minimal makeup when she finishes her hair, accentuating her beauty. Aubrey is glowing up her skin with shea butter when she receives a call from Lily.

"What's up, Lil?" Aubrey answers.

"Please tell me you aren't wearing your green dress. I need to borrow it!" Lily's voice is dramatically desperate.

"Of course, it's all yours."

"Thank you!" she appreciates sincerely. "I'll be there in two point five." Lily ends the call before Aubrey can respond.

Smiling and shaking her head, Aubrey tosses the phone aside. She scans over the pile of clothes on her futon, contemplating which dress to wear. Putting on a blue dress, she realizes its length does not suit her. Next, she tries on a red dress and is uncomfortable with how tight it is. Finally, she slips on a black dress. It fits her flawlessly. She pairs the dress with strappy heels and gathers her things when she hears a knock on the door.

"Come in," she calls out while rummaging through the pile of clothes, looking for her phone and purse.

Aubrey glances over her shoulder, expecting her dark-haired, green-eyed best friend, but instead, it is her handsome heavenly neighbor. Daniel stands in her doorway, elegantly dressed in a suit tailored to perfection over his muscles. His fresh haircut, paired with a precisely trimmed beard, is shining. In general, he is a nice-looking man, but the extra effort he puts into his appearance increases his appeal. Her gaze dances over his tall frame, taking in the king gracing her apartment. They don't speak a word to each other, but their silent communication speaks volumes. Daniel's shallow breathing communicates that Aubrey is taking his breath away. Aubrey's engaged stare conveys that Daniel is the focus of her concentration. Finally, she invites him in with her eyes, and he steps inside, closing the door behind him.

Once inside, Daniel still doesn't state his reason for knocking on her door. Instead, he waits, allowing his presence to make the statement. Aubrey can feel his masculine energy. He is there to establish authority as the leading male in her life. She respects it. Secretly, it brings her excitement. She leans against the wall, bracing herself for whatever Daniel has in store for her. "What are you doing here?"

Daniel closes the distance between them, putting his hand against the wall so that she is between it and his body. The intimate proximity starts the heat. He travels his eyes over the black dress that hardly covers her abundant curves, weakening him. He has never seen her outside of her sports clothes. The dress and heels are stunning on her. His eyes roam freely, beholding the immaculate art before him. "You look … mmm … like a goddess, a freaking masterpiece." He admits while staying confident as if her date with Jace is nothing to him. "But you already know that."

"You're right. I know." She matches his certainty.

"I think that dress is more than your little friend can handle."

"Why are you concerned with what Jace can handle?"

"Because you're mine," Daniel replies, his confidence skyrocketing to a delusional altitude.

Aubrey drags her eyes over him from head to toe, pretending she isn't dripping with desire for him. "I belong to the one who formed me in my mother's womb, and that's it."

"What if he formed you for me?" Aubrey blinks, and Daniel continues. "You're my soulmate, and you know it." He shifts his hand from the wall to lean on his forearm, bringing their faces just inches apart. "I came to tell you how much I miss you," he whispers transparently.

"I miss you so much," Aubrey admits faintly, exposing her true feelings. She steps closer to him, forcing their bodies together. She reaches up, wrapping her arms around his neck, and he eagerly returns her touch, enclosing her in his arms. As always, she feels his lips brush against her neck, but there is something different about feeling his lips on her body this time. It feels like her skin is on fire but not burning. Loving the feeling, Aubrey tilts her head to give him more access. Daniel goes to work, his lips delicately caressing her skin until she becomes putty in his hands. His lips move from her neck to her jawline, then to her cheek. Finally, he stops after kissing the corner of her mouth.

"We're not going to the fashion show tonight," he declares. Aubrey wills herself to say something, anything, but she is stuck. She knows what she should do—tell Daniel to leave because her mind isn't functioning correctly. His kisses have her body, heart, and mind in a whirlwind. She doesn't exactly know what he meant by, *We're not going to the fashion show tonight*. If they aren't going, what are they going to do? If things continue to progress, she knows that they will do everything. Is she willing to do everything with him? It is too much to consider, and the moment feels too intense to waste on thinking. Instead of speaking, Aubrey parts her lips, exhales slowly, and lifts her chin toward him. Daniel meets her halfway, bending down until their foreheads touch. He breathes into her open mouth, eager to finally have her. His minty breath, mixed with the aroma of his cologne, nearly intoxicates Aubrey. Her eyes flutter to a close as she locks her arms tighter around his neck. She moves in closer, bringing their noses together. The closeness is all Daniel needs to interpret that she is on the same page as him. He presses his mouth against hers, preparing to devour her lips, but the sound of the door hitting the wall makes Aubrey jump out of his arms. Daniel and Aubrey look over to see Lily's wide eyes and open mouth.

"Oh! Um. I'll just get my green dress and be on my way," Lily offers.

Able to think clearly, Aubrey scurries into her bathroom to escape from Daniel. "I'll see you there, Daniel," Aubrey calls out as she runs off.

Huffing out a disappointed sigh, Daniel leaves Aubrey's apartment, closing the door.

Lily rushes to the bathroom behind Aubrey, excitement gleaming over her face. "Girl!"

Aubrey has her face in her hands. "What is wrong with me?" she groans, replaying how she almost relinquished all of herself on a whim.

Chapter Eleven

AUBREY AND LILY walk into the fashion show venue. A long runway is in the middle of the room, and on each side of the runway are seven tables adorned with confetti balloons and V.I.P. place cards. Aubrey scans the empty tables, looking for her and Jace's name cards. Instead, she finds her reservation next to Daniel's card. Aubrey picks up Daniel's card and switches it out with Jace's at a different table. "What are you doing?" Lily asks.

Aubrey doesn't answer. She smoothly slides into her seat as if everything is normal. Seconds later, Daniel seemingly appears out of thin air, holding his name card. He glances at Aubrey with a perplexed expression as he switches his name card back to its original place. "What's up?" he asks, his tone full of questions as he sits in the seat next to her.

"Hey," Aubrey replies awkwardly, avoiding the question and his eyes. Being close to him is still electrifying. It is as if she can still feel his lips on her neck and the tingling it produces in her body. She jumps to her feet in a panic. "Be right back." She looks around the room desperately for an escape. Aubrey's gaze lands on Jace entering the venue. Before she can stop, she carries herself in his direction.

"What's up with your girl?" Daniel asks Lily.

Lily waves her hand, diminishing Daniel's concern. "Just Aubrey being Aubrey. Y'all's almost-moment alarmed her. Now she's running like a wild Tennessee dog from every feeling she's ever felt for you."

Daniel's brown eyes turn dark. "She's running? But I just got her back!"

Daniel sees red. The red doesn't derive from anger but from revenge. A revenge dress, in fact. Jade's red dress gloriously grips her body. She switches her hips toward Daniel, proud of her body's power. Daniel locks in on her approach, influenced by her feminine supremacy. Jade's extraordinary beauty captures his attention and makes him uneasy. She stops in front of him, mocking him with all her glory. An awkward and feverish moment lingers between them before she laughs. "Karma must have your location." She glances over her shoulder at Aubrey and then back to Daniel before walking away, shaking her head while wearing the smuggest smirk.

Daniel and Lily look at Aubrey across the room as she throws her arms around Jace. Daniel's jaw clenches, a pulsing vein visible on the side of his head. He explodes from his chair. Lily reacts quickly, grabbing his arm. "Let me handle it," she says, reasoning with him.

Across the room, Aubrey shamelessly flirts with Jace. She smiles at him while hanging on to his arm. Jace's mind is going wild. He always wanted to get close to Aubrey in every way, but she had never given him the opportunity. Jace hooks his arm around her waist and pulls her close. "What are you trying to do to me right now? Don't play with me," he says into her ear.

Aubrey brushes off his comment with a playful tap on the arm. "You're so funny." She giggles. Jace turns on the full force of his eyes, ready for his king-charming act causing Aubrey to cringe. Thankfully, Lily intervenes just in time.

"Hi, Jace. I need to borrow my friend." Lily takes Aubrey's hand and pulls her to the restroom. Once they have privacy, Lily releases Aubrey's hand and crosses her arms. She glares sternly, and Aubrey stares back innocently and unbothered.

"You were just about to surrender it all to Daniel, and now you're hugged up with your ex in Daniel's face. That is so wrong," Lily accuses.

"Jace was just a friend!" Aubrey corrects, exasperated.

"Yeah, you keep trying to sell that story, but nobody's buying it. I'm just trying to figure out if your history is repeating itself. Jace was just a friend. Daniel is just a friend..."

"I don't owe Daniel anything," Aubrey lashes out. "Let's not forget there are things I don't know about him."

Lily massages her temple as if Aubrey is giving her a headache. "You treat everyone like they're coming to take something from you, even when they're just trying to give you love. It's exhausting!" Lily exits the bathroom without another word.

Aubrey strolls back into the venue with her eyes on the floor. She silently slides into her seat, careful not to make eye contact with Daniel. She looks around the room for Jace. He is sitting at a table surrounded by beautiful women. He shrugs innocently, letting Aubrey know he has no control over the seating arrangements. Aubrey can tell that he has no complaints about his placement. When Aubrey turns away, he leans closer to the woman beside him. "What are you trying to do to me right now? Don't play with me," he whispers in her ear.

On stage, a band is playing a jazzy musical selection. Closing her eyes, Aubrey allows the saxophone to carry her away. After a while, Travis' voice on the microphone interrupts her moment of peace. "Next up, we have a good friend of mine sharing some spoken word. Welcome, Daniel Sane, to the stage."

An uneasy feeling drops in Aubrey's stomach. He hadn't told her that he was participating in the show. Intuition reveals that she is the reason for his stage appearance. Refusing to acknowledge him, Aubrey looks at the floor and pretends he doesn't exist. Daniel walks on stage and stands in front of the mic. He looks directly at Aubrey. "Sad song or love song?" he questions into the microphone, his voice carrying through the room. The question causes Aubrey to stiffen. Her eyes fly open, giving him her undivided attention. Once he has what he wants, Daniel continues.

"I'm not sure.
Frankly, the mystery is a lot to endure.

A Small Piece Of Her Heart

One verse you desperately need me.
The next, you're hopelessly leaving me.

I'm not sure what you want from me.
I am sure I want you to sing to me.

Sing me your fears. Sing me your pain.
Sing me your hopes. Sing me insane.

A cappella, raise your voice while I connect with you.
Bring back the beat as I lay next to you.

I need you to sing, my love.
I can't seem to stop falling in love.

This is a love song, right?
If I'm wrong, the sky is not blue.

If the sky is not blue, neither is the ocean.
If the ocean isn't either, the sun does not shine.
And if the sun doesn't shine…

No, this can't be a sad song … right?

Sad song. Love song. Whatever you want it to be.
It's your choice, just don't stop singing to me.

Because I crave your music. I crave your song.
You crave me too. I dare you to tell me I'm not wrong.

I'll unlock my secrets and leave nothing to mystery.
Just enlighten me. Is this a sad song or a love song you
sing to me?"

The room is entirely silent for what feels like an eternity as Daniel infiltrates Aubrey from the stage, and she speechlessly gapes back at him. For a moment, no one else exists but the two of them. Thundering applause from the audience breaks the silence. Aubrey quickly swipes her hand across her face, hiding the evidence of the lone tear escaping down her cheek. From the corner of her eye, she sees Jace rise from his table and exit the venue. A long sigh escapes her as remorse takes precedence, and she regrets every decision in the last forty-eight hours.

AUBREY LEANS AGAINST the elevator wall, emotionally exhausted from the evening. In her mind, she plans to kick off her heels and fall into bed as soon as she steps into her apartment. As soon as the elevator doors open, she finds Daniel standing in front of her door.

She releases a tired sigh. "Let's talk about it tomorrow."

"What's the problem now, Aubrey?" he asks, frustrated.

"I said I'll talk to you tomorrow." Aubrey waits for him to move away from her door, but he stands his ground.

"I'll play your game as long as you want, but don't make me feel like I'm losing," he says roughly.

Aubrey's hands flail out. "I don't know what you're talking about."

"You're not going to play in my face. Flirting and hugging up on another dude."

Taking a step back, Aubrey checks him with a look. "Don't be mad when you start a game, and I know how to play as well as you." Daniel scowls at her, and she scowls back. "You used Jade to try to hurt me. That doesn't make me feel safe."

"Instead of communicating that with me, you did the same thing to hurt me."

Aubrey rolls her eyes. "You're right; I did."

"Okay," he speaks with a frustrated sigh. Pinching the bridge of his nose, he drops his head. "I apologize, Aubrey. What I did wasn't the right thing." His following words come out so softly they are practically inaudible. "I just love you. I'm trying to figure out what to do about it."

Aubrey feels all her irritation with him exit her body, leaving nothing but compassion for him. Finally, she releases a long exhale. "Can I be honest about something?"

He lifts one shoulder and lets it drop carelessly, not wanting to hear her honesty. Instead, he only wants to hear that she loves him back.

"Being with you is an escape for me," Aubrey says. "It's a secluded island that's beautiful, serene, and easy. But it's just a vacation, and I can't stop thinking about home, which is a mess. I could enjoy the vacation much better if I cleaned up at home first."

"That mess is not your home," he voices passionately. "The beauty, serenity, and bliss that you feel within when you're still is your home. It's our home. How amazing would it be if we got to experience that every day together?"

Aubrey can't deny that he is right; she longs to reside in that home eternally. She knows she can have peace anywhere as long as she has peace within. Still, for some reason, she struggles to release her physical home. "Can you do me a favor and be patient with me?" she requests softly.

"I'd do anything for you, Aubrey," he professes earnestly.

Aubrey feels a gentle flutter in her gut while looking into his eyes, seeing that he means every word. She opens her arms to embrace him, and he gladly accepts. Closing her eyes, she rests her head on his shoulder, breathing in his scent and soaking up his touch. During their time apart, she mostly missed how secure she felt in his arms, how perfectly she seemed to fit with his body. She hadn't realized how much she looked forward to his daily hugs until she didn't have them anymore. They stand in the hallway hugging for an extended moment before Aubrey pushes up on her tiptoes, putting her lips close to his ear. "And just so you know, it's definitely a love song," she acknowledges quietly. "And not the kind that stops me from breathing. You feel like fresh air after confinement."

Chapter Twelve

DANIEL AND AUBREY BECOME inseparable again. Daniel accompanies Aubrey at four in the morning to experience home alongside her. They sit side by side on yoga mats, still breathing until they find peace within and mental clarity. After sitting still for so long, Aubrey begins stretching to awaken her body. Daniel attempts to follow her stretching routine, but it becomes too advanced once she releases her feet to stand on her hands. Finally, Daniel concedes and finds new peace in watching Aubrey, admiring her strength and beauty in the moonlight. To him, she is flawless, the epitome of pure beauty. He would have been content to watch her every move his entire day.

After finishing their morning routine, they ride together to campus, singing and dancing in the car. When they have a break in the day, they send videos of Daniel's races to his dream agent. Then they take a nap together. In the evening, the two of them rest on the sofa. Daniel lies on Aubrey's chest, using her as his pillow while she rubs her fingers throughout his scalp.

He keeps looking at a laundry basket full of clothes across the room that he needs to tend to, but the feeling of her fingers massaging his head is too soothing, and her body is too soft and warm to depart from. "Maybe if you stop rubbing me, I could get up," he mumbles lazily. Aubrey's fingers stop moving. "Nooo, don't stop," he complains.

Aubrey giggles. "Go get the clothes. I'll help you fold," she offers, pushing him off her.

Daniel rolls to his feet and retrieves the laundry basket. Aubrey reaches inside, taking out a jersey. Holding it up, she examines it. It has his last name printed in bold letters and the number fourteen. "Your college jersey," Aubrey muses while sliding the jersey over her head. "I'm keeping it, and when you're a famous NFL star, I'll find you and make you autograph it for me."

Daniel shrugs. "You can keep it, but you're not going to have to find me. You'll wear it to bed in our home whenever I'm a famous NFL star." Daniel studies her expression, seeing a smile take up her face as she pictures herself wearing his jersey around their home. She doesn't say anything. Instead, she just picks up another shirt and folds it. Daniel also opts out of saying another word. He has planted the seed and will give it time to grow. In between folding each item, he peeks over to check on her. She chews on her lip while staring into oblivion. He hopes she is deeply daydreaming about sharing her life with him.

The sound of Daniel's phone ringing takes his focus away from Aubrey. Checking his screen, he reads the word *Mama* and eagerly answers the call. "Mama! What up, girl?" He puts the call on speakerphone and sets the phone on the couch between Aubrey and himself.

In the background of the call, Daniel and Aubrey hear waves crashing over tranquil music.

"Not much," Sylvia answers, her tone just as tranquil as the music. "Daddy treated me to a spa day. I just finished a massage. My facial is next, but I wanted to return your call first."

"Don't let me interrupt. I didn't want anything. I was just calling to hear your voice earlier." Aubrey places her palms together, resting her cheek on the top of her hand. Her eyes fill with admiration as she experiences Daniel talking to his mother.

"You are such a sweetheart. What are you up to?"

"Just hanging with Aubrey. My Bree Bree. She's helping me fold clothes."

The call gets quiet for a moment. "Your Bree Bree? And when did Aubrey get a nickname?" Sylvia questions, her tone no longer tranquil.

"I just decided to call her that," Daniel explains. He looks at Aubrey, gently flicking the tip of her nose.

"Hmmm," Sylvia replies in a stale manner.

Daniel chuckles. "Don't do it, Mom. I hear you starting to worry when there is nothing to worry about."

"You know I expect you to focus on your studies and career. I'd be disappointed if you got some girl pregnant before she became your wife. Remember what I taught you about chastity."

"You told me that since I was twelve, and I've been listening. Besides, this girl won't let me touch her anyway. I just want to kiss on her a little bit."

Aubrey's mouth drops open.

"Daniel!" Sylvia says his name firmly.

Daniel bursts into laughter. "I'm just messing with you, Mom."

"Boy! I got to go. I'll call you tonight," Sylvia says.

"I'll wait up for you. Love you, love you, love you."

"Love you, Honey."

Daniel taps his screen to end the call.

"Why would you say that to your mom?" Aubrey throws a pair of socks in his direction. He catches the socks before they hit him in the face and wrestles Aubrey down until he hovers over her, staring at her lips.

"I'm just telling the truth."

"You better listen to your mom's advice," Aubrey warns, putting her hand in his face and pushing him off her. She becomes still and pensive. "Wonder what advice my mom would give me about you," she ponders aloud.

"You should call her."

One solid laugh rings out. "And ask her if I can lay in her lap while she gives her best mommy dearest advice?" she comments facetiously.

"Yeah, if that's what you want," Daniel replies.

Aubrey pauses, noting that his tone is void of humor. His suggestion appalls her. "Why? Why would I sacrifice my dignity for someone who purposely put up a barrier?"

"People make mistakes sometimes, Bree."

"And people need to be held accountable for their mistakes."

"What do you want from your mom? Do you want a relationship or reparations?" Daniel challenges.

The answer is obvious.

SHE STANDS ALONE in her apartment. Aubrey blankly eyes the word *mom* in her contact list. She hovers her thumb over the call button, hesitating. She can't come up with words to say to her mother after five years of not speaking. Should she act like everything is normal or demand answers and healing? Aubrey closes her eyes, not allowing herself to think about it any longer. She sucks in a breath and lets it seep out slowly. She inhales again, feeling the air take up space, and relaxes her body as she exhales. Aubrey breathes in one final time. "Just do it," she tells herself, then releases her thumb onto the screen, pushing the call button. Once she hears the phone ringing, her heart thumps speedily in anticipation. It is hard to differentiate between the sound of the phone ringing from the ringing in her ears. She stands stiff and rigid, holding her breath.

"Hello?" Nia's voice transmits through the receiver.

Aubrey throws her hand over her lips, stunned by the familiar demure voice. The gentle sound of one word from her mouth brings Aubrey's eyes fluttering to a close and tears seeping out. "Hi," she breathes. "It's me, Aubrey."

A peaceful moment passes before her mother replies. "Aubrey! Hey sweetie," Nia greets, her voice trembling. "Wow. How are you?"

"I'm doing good," she sniffles through her words.

Neither of them speaks for a moment, but it feels normal. Aubrey's mother is a woman of few words. Most of what she says is communicated through her smiles, hugs, and kisses. "What have you been up to?" Aubrey asks.

"Oh, just gardening," she answers. Aubrey can picture her mother in front of the house, on her knees, digging in the dirt. It was what she did almost daily after cooking breakfast and folding laundry. "What about you?"

"I'm still running. I got a scholarship," Aubrey informs.

"I heard about that. I see Lily's mom at the market every now and then. She always gives me a good report. She says you're a really great runner."

Aubrey's almond-shaped eyes turn round when she hears that Mrs. Landers has been keeping Nia updated on her. "Really?" Aubrey notes. "Well, maybe one day I'll see you in the stands. I'm sure Mrs. Landers wouldn't mind you riding with her." Aubrey holds her breath as she waits for her mom's response to her subtle invite.

"I would love that," Nia tells her enthusiastically. "When is your next race?"

Her mom's enthusiasm gives Aubrey renewed vitality in the lifeless parts of her heart. "I have a track meet this weekend. Do you think you can make it?"

"If I can catch a ride with Lily's mom, I'll be there," she assures Aubrey.

Tears roll down Aubrey's cheeks simultaneously as the corners of her mouth lift into the broadest smile. "I'll call Mrs. Landers and set everything up."

"I'll be ready!"

A comfortable silence lingers over the call for another beat. "Mom?" Aubrey calls after a minute. "I'm looking forward to hugging you."

"You have no idea how much I'm looking forward to this," her mom speaks softly and sincerely.

THAT WEEKEND inside the arena, the stands are packed. The mile run is happening on the track while Aubrey, Daniel, Lily, and Travis warm up in the middle of the field. Coach Aaron walks by, giving them an excited fist bump. When he gets to Aubrey, he stands in front of her with his fist out. Ignoring his fist, Aubrey dodges to the side to keep her eyes on the door. She sighs when she sees the people walking through aren't an older version of Lily and herself. "Where are they?" Aubrey whines.

"I talked to my mom a couple hours ago, and she said she was on her way to pick up your mom," Lily says, eyeing the door along with Aubrey.

Just as Lily finishes her sentence, Mrs. Landers walks through the door. She stands with her hand on the door, holding it for the person walking in after her. Aubrey takes off running in a full sprint. Lily is right on her heels. Once Aubrey gets to where Mrs. Landers stands, she can see who Lily's mom is holding the door for—a couple with four small children. Aubrey looks past the couple towing the children for her mother's face, but there isn't anyone there. Turning toward Mrs. Landers, Aubrey reads the remorseful expression on her face.

"What happened?" Aubrey questions emotionally.

Mrs. Landers mashes her lips together as if she doesn't want to say.

"Is she okay?" Aubrey asks in a panic.

Mrs. Landers nods. "When I got there, she was gardening. She said she couldn't come because she got off schedule and didn't finish all her chores."

"Gardening in January," Aubrey questions dubiously.

Mrs. Landers raises her shoulders, not able to offer any logic.

"Didn't finish her chores," Aubrey repeats, primarily to herself. She imagines her mother kneeling in the frozen garden instead of in the stands. Aubrey feels insignificant, like she doesn't actually exist. Her entire being must be a mirage, a dream, a figment of her imagination. Nothing else makes sense.

Lily reaches out to rub Aubrey's arm.

"I'm good," Aubrey says, convincing herself and refusing to allow it to affect her. Everything goes blurry as tears are disloyal to Aubrey's resolve. Walking away, Aubrey wipes her eyes and returns to the middle of the turf to finish warming up for her race.

"Is she here?" Daniel asks.

Aubrey shrugs dismissively and walks past him. Her eyes emotionless as she robotically finishes the stretch routine. When it is time for her race, she takes her lane on the track and gets into her starting blocks. The umpire raises his hand and fires the gun. Aubrey takes off running. As she runs, her body feels weighed down. Her feet move slowly as if they know they are running without purpose, leading her nowhere.

The blank expression remains on Aubrey's face as she walks away from the finish line to the winner's podium to watch Jade collect the gold medal while she receives an eighth-place ribbon. Jade jumps up and down on the podium, hyped about her win. Jade poses for photos with cocky superiority. Lily stands in the number two spot, looking down at Aubrey with concern. Aubrey simply gazes at the cameras without a smile. The moment the photographer lowers his camera, Aubrey bolts out of the arena.

Chapter Thirteen

DANIEL STANDS IN FRONT of Aubrey's apartment door, holding a gift bag with one hand and knocking with the other. At first, his knocks are light taps. After five minutes pass, and he still doesn't get an answer from her, he pounds on the wood impatiently. "Let me in, Bree," he pleads from the outside. A few more minutes pass without a response before he decides to try the knob. He turns it, and it grants him access. He finds Aubrey lying across her futon, her knees to her chest, just staring at the wall.

"Hey," Daniel calls out.

Aubrey remains unresponsive. Daniel stands in her line of sight, attempting to force her to acknowledge him. Instead, she simply stares through him.

Reaching into the gift bag, Daniel pulls out a package of command strips, followed by a large photo frame. He attaches the command strips to the back of the frame and presses it against Aubrey's empty wall. Next, he steps to the side so that Aubrey can see it. The photo frame is a collage with the word family scribed in big letters across the top. Daniel had filled the collage with memories of the two of them—Aubrey and Daniel eating from one plate at Trav's cookout—paparazzi courtesy of Lily, the two of them sporting gold medals at his first track meet, a photo from their date at the arcade, and random selfies they had taken in his apartment. Every image is evidence of the bond they had established during their months together.

"I'm your family," he proclaims with steadfast loyalty.

Still, Aubrey doesn't react. She's looking at the photos, but Daniel can't tell if she is actually seeing them. As he climbs onto the futon, he presses his forehead against hers. He leans in to softly caress her cheeks with his lips. Aubrey remains entirely still, as if she can't feel anything internally or externally. "Can you tell me what you're thinking," he requests in a hushed voice.

Aubrey gives him her eyes. They are eerily desolate. The skin around them is gray and dry. Daniel feels like he is staring into the face of a corpse. Without warning, Aubrey leans into Daniel's neck and begins working her mouth over his skin. Her lips are aggressive and cold. The feeling holds no appeal. Taking her face in his hands, he gently guides her mouth away from him. Aubrey pulls her shirt over her head, tossing it to the floor. She tugs on the bottom elastic in her sports bra, preparing to remove it. Daniel hurries to wrap his fingers around her wrists, immobilizing her arms. "What are you doing, Bree Bree?" he questions with a frustrated, gruff voice.

"I'm done caring about everything." She leans toward his mouth, making Daniel release her wrists to take hold of her face again. With her hands free,

A Small Piece Of Her Heart

Aubrey grabs his shirt hem, trying to pull it over his head.

Daniel grabs her hands again, locking them in place. "I won't let you self-destruct because you're hurt. What happened to the confident goddess who has standards higher than heaven?"

She shrugs carelessly. "I don't care anymore. Just help me feel better." Lying flat on the futon, Aubrey creates an opportunity for Daniel to do whatever pleases him. She gives Daniel permission to make her forget that there's a world outside the two of them. All the beauty in the world couldn't make him rise. Aubrey's abrupt neglect of self-worth is saddening. "Let's go," Daniel demands. He gets up from the futon and scoops Aubrey into his arms. He carries her into the bathroom, standing in front of the mirror. "Look at yourself."

Aubrey gazes at her reflection in the mirror. The sunken eyes and pale skin cause her heart to pound frantically. She doesn't recognize herself, which torments her further as she realizes that she is becoming unrecognizable from the inside out. The burning begins in her nose, and moisture fills her eyes. "Why can't I just get over it!" she burst out. "It's been five years, and I still feel like such a mess inside!" Daniel wraps his arms around her, holding onto her from behind. "You are not a robot, babe." He sighs. "I know what it's like to be a mess, too," he admits, his voice deep and piercing. "I'm telling you this only because I think you need to hear it, and I trust you not to repeat it." He feels Aubrey's body go rigid in his arms. He peeks up to see her curious stare reflecting from the mirror. "Earlier this year, my mom got bad news from her doctor. "He said she had 6 months to live. I couldn't fathom it, so I started drinking to numb the anxiety. Eventually, I lost control. I would wake up and not know what day it was.

"My grades dropped. I was drunk at football practice. My coaches tried, but they had no choice but to let me go. I left Texas and went home to North Carolina. I remember seeing my mom for the first time since she had been sick. Her frailty took my breath away. I downed another bottle.

"One day, I woke up in a hospital after Kennedy found me passed out in my car. I had been in there for a couple of hours. It was extremely hot that day, so I was in bad shape. After that, my dad forced me to go to rehab. It's why I missed out on football season. I spent 3 months in the facility. They told me to repeat that I was an addict, which made me feel like I'd never move on from that experience.

My mom started searching for different healing solutions. She found a woman specializing in mental wellness. She gave us a strategy to realign from the inside out. We committed to doing her plan together. I left rehab, and my mom started holistic healing. We started feeling better. Then, I applied to this university. I wanted to surround myself with mental elevation. That way I could center myself spiritually while getting back in shape physically."

"Do you mind sharing the strategy with me?" she inquires.

"Of course. The plan consists of a series of things starting with changing our mindsets to believe in what some people may call impossible. My mom is going to live no matter what those doctors say. That is what she chooses to believe, and I choose to believe with her. Once we believe, we change the words we speak. Life and death are in the power of the tongue, right? Well, we decided to only speak life over our situations. So my mom's not claiming sickness or death, and I'm no longer speaking about my past mistakes. I am not an addict. I've turned every mistake into a lesson, and that man is not who I am. I overcame my stuff, just like you will overcome everything you're going through. That's the only reason I'm speaking about this—to help you return to where you belong. Remember your true lineage. You come from so much greater than what you were birthed into. You are here to put heaven on earth. You have all that divine power inside of you to restore generations. I need you to remember who you are. You are a real-life goddess."

His words restore the life in Aubrey's eyes as she remembers her worth. She wipes her tears, feeling renewed. "Thank you," she says, in awe of him.

Daniel takes her hand and leads her back to the living room. Retrieving her shirt from the floor, he places it over her head and helps guide her arms through the sleeves. They sit on the futon and relax back, resting their heads on Aubrey's single pillow. Aubrey wraps her arms around one of Daniel's arms, soaking in his touch. She desires more of him, so she hooks her leg over his legs, pulling him closer. Using his free hand, Daniel reaches over to run his hand up and down her back. Securely snuggled, Aubrey closes her eyes and doesn't open them until the following day.

Sunlight dances through her lashes as she peels her eyes open. The first sight she sees is Daniel's smiling brown eyes sparkling in the light.

"Morning." His deep voice vibrates through her.

"Good morning," she echoes.

Still snuggled in the same position as the night before, they lay motionless, reflecting on the transformation between them. Daniel had committed to being her family, and Aubrey had committed to allowing him to be that for her. They don't feel the need to establish it with words or define it with a title. The bond and connection are enough for them.

"Being with you feels like breathing fresh air," Aubrey whispers. Daniel's eyes flutter to a close. Aubrey moves her hands from around his arm to gently take his face in her hands. She slowly inches forward until she is nose-to-nose with him. She delicately presses her mouth against his soft lips, giving him the sweetest peck on the lips. She returns to her place on the pillow, a peaceful smile coloring her lips. That small taste of her warmth and sweetness leaves Daniel hungry for more. He contains himself, knowing that she requires his restrained intimacy for the time being. So, they rest. Completely still. Breathing each other in. Immersed in each other's eyes.

In the middle of their stillness, Daniel's phone rings. He reluctantly releases her gaze to check the phone. A number he doesn't recognize flashes across the screen. He scrutinizes the number, thinking deeply about whether he should answer. Ultimately, he slides his thumb across the screen and answers the call.

"Hello?"

The voice on the other end begins speaking. Daniel shoots up into a sitting position. Alarmed, Aubrey sits up too. She watches Daniel's eyes frantically scan the room until they land on her journal. He reaches his long arms across her body and snatches it up. He takes the pen from the spiral binding, opens it to a blank page, and begins writing. Aubrey strains her neck to see what he is scribbling on the page. She sees the words *quit track* and *Monday morning*.

"Absolutely," Daniel speaks into the phone as his hand moves speedily. "Sure, I look forward to meeting you." Daniel ends the call and then jumps to his feet, letting out a joyful howl. He jumps up and down while waving his hands over his head.

Aubrey jumps up, too, and begins rejoicing with him. "What are we celebrating?" she asks.

"That was Grant Lennox. He said he's been following my career since high school. He got the videos we sent and said my times are impressive." Daniel jumps again and releases another shout. "He wants to discuss how he can get me an invite to the combine. We're going to set up a meeting to discuss specifics, and if everything sounds right for me, I'll start training for the combine."

"You have to quit track?" she asks.

"I can't sign with an agent while still being an amateur athlete."

An ear-to-ear smile grows over her face. "A professional athlete! I'll miss my teammate, but I am super proud of you."

MONDAY MORNING, Daniel walks into a conference building, preparing to meet with Grant Lennox. His sister is by his side, devoted to being his support system. Kennedy lightly taps his hand to stop him from fidgeting with the tie around his neck.

"You look great," she assures him.

"Thanks," he replies, his tone subdued.

The two of them enter the lobby and encounter two familiar faces. Daniel freezes when he sees his mother, mostly because she looks entirely different since he last saw her.

"Surprise!" Sylvia yells. "You didn't think we'd miss your big moment, did you?" Daniel continues staring at his mom with an open mouth. "Oh yeah, and I gained thirty pounds," she announces proudly while twirling in a circle.

Daniel grabs his mother and squeezes her tightly. Seeing her healthy made all the bad seem like nothing more than a faint memory. "We're doing it, mom. We're living," he whispers, growing emotional. Daniel's dad joins the hug, followed by Kennedy. The four of them embrace in the lobby for a lengthy precious moment.

"Daniel Sane?" a man in an immaculate suit calls out. Daniel wipes the few tears that escaped before turning to greet the agent. "My name is Grant Lennox. It's a pleasure," he says while shaking Daniel's hand. "Follow me." Grant leads Daniel and his family to a conference room. They sit down at a long wooden table. "Here is the vision I have for you," Grant tells Daniel and then proceeds to pitch a plan for his NFL career. Daniel listens more than he speaks and takes time to read over the details of each paper Grant puts in front of him.

When Grant finishes speaking, Daniel takes out his Plan Book. Inside is a set of documents. Daniel hands them to Grant. "Here is the vision I have for myself."

Grant reads the documents, taking time to consider the details. "Alright," he says once he finishes. "I respect this, but I'll need you down in Texas for training when you sign."

"Why Texas?" Daniel inquires.

"That's where the best trainers are. You haven't

played in a while, and we need to make up for lost time."

Daniel calculates the amount of time between training and the combine. "So, I'd be in Texas for three months?"

Grant nods. "And then Indianapolis, and then back to Texas."

"No more Ohio?" His voice cracks as the words escape his lips.

"The moment you sign, we're done with Ohio." Daniel stares across at him with eyes full of apprehension. "Take some time and think it over," Grant says before ending the meeting and exiting the conference room.

Once Grant is gone, Daniel takes out his phone to text Aubrey.

"What are you doing?" his mom asks.

"Reaching out to Aubrey," he replies simply.

His dad, mom, and sister give him the same incredulous look. "Is that why you're hesitating on a dream you've had since you were a young boy?" his dad asks. "Ever since you met her, your focus has been off."

Daniel looks up from his phone, perplexed. His dad's concern bewilders Daniel. "I'm about to graduate with an engineering degree and sign with my dream agent. So how is my focus off?"

His dad's jaw tightens as he scoots to the edge of his seat. Sylvia puts her hand on her husband's leg, patting it. "I think your dad is saying that this girl occupies a lot of your attention," Sylvia explains. "Kennedy says you don't answer her calls, and she doesn't see much of you anymore."

Daniel eyes Kennedy. She lifts her shoulders and lets them drop unapologetically. "Is it not the truth?"

Sylvia reaches across the table to take her son's hand. She strokes it gently. "This family is in the middle of a fight for our lives. You and Kennedy need to stick together."

Feeling like he is in the middle of an ambush intervention meeting, Daniel stands from his seat and looks each of them in the eyes one by one. "Stop." He decisively puts his foot down. "I'm not pushing Kennedy away. I met a girl and fell in love. I'm allowed to do that." He has been doing his best to live a life he is proud of, and he refuses to let them strip away his honor.

"In love?" Sylvia repeats, exasperated. Kennedy rolls her eyes while Delmain glares in his direction.

"And where is this girl? Why haven't we met her?" Delmain demands.

"Kennedy met her," Daniel says, hoping they would let him off the hook.

"And I didn't like her." Kennedy offers her unconcealed disapproval.

"Kennedy!" Daniel calls out in disappointment, knowing that her opinion holds a lot of weight with their parents.

Kennedy doesn't waiver. "I didn't like how she was hounding you about why you weren't playing football. It's none of her business."

Grinding his teeth together, Daniel glares at his sister.

"You didn't tell her, did you?" Sylvia questions.

Daniel mashes his lips together and crosses his arms. Delmain, Kennedy, and Sylvia all jump to their feet at the same time.

"Are you crazy?" Kennedy yells.

"What if she sells the story to the press," Delmain throws out.

"We agreed that we weren't going to speak about it!" Sylvia reminds him, displeasure heavy in her tone.

Daniel can't stand to see the disappointment in his mother's eyes. He looks down at the floor, soaking in guilt.

"We need to meet this girl as soon as possible," Delmain demands.

AFTER HIS MEETING, the first thing Daniel does is knock on Aubrey's door. After only one knock, the door flies open. "Did you sign?" Aubrey asks eagerly.

He answers with a nod. "Guess what?"

"What?"

"My parents are in town, and my mom is cooking a celebratory dinner," he states slyly. "I want you to come."

Still high off the moment, she agrees easily. "I'd love to."

Chapter Fourteen

DANIEL AND AUBREY ARRIVE at his sister's place, where his parents are staying for the week. He drives the car into the driveway of a modestly sized townhome tucked away in a gated community. Aubrey notes how all the homes line up in a perfect row, having the same tidy and inviting look. Of course, she thinks to herself, this is precisely the kind of atmosphere she would've predicted an entitled brash woman like Kennedy would lay her head at night. She pictures the women in the neighborhood exiting their homes to collect the mail at the end of the driveway wearing stilettos that cost more than their rent. "You ready?" Daniel asks, his voice a bit unsteady. Aubrey's brows scrunch together, detecting his nervousness.

"I'm ready," she says. "Are you?"

"Of course," he declares, feigning confidence.

Daniel pushes the button to turn off the car and exits, walking around to the passenger side to open Aubrey's door. He takes her hand, holding her tightly as he guides her to the front door. Daniel turns the knob and walks inside. His mom, dad, and sister are standing nearby waiting for them. Aubrey feels suffocated the moment she sees their faces. They all look at her with the same curious expression, as if they have a planned list of questions ready to unleash on her.

Daniel's dad speaks first. "I am so happy to finally meet you, Aubrey." He is tall, very handsome, and lying through his thick South African accent. He isn't happy to meet her; she can sense his disapproval through the robotic hug he offers.

"You as well," Aubrey replies, doing her best not to cringe away from his touch.

Sylvia approaches Aubrey next, giving her a gentle hug and kiss. "Hi, Aubrey. Welcome!"

"Thank you."

Aubrey watches as Sylvia moves on to greet her son. The way she hugs and kisses Daniel has much more warmth and generosity. It is obvious to Aubrey that Daniel's family is working hard to be on their best behavior as if they have already decided not to like her. Looking away, Aubrey notices Kennedy standing in the background, staring. Kennedy's eyes sparkle with excitement as a devious smile glows over her face. Kennedy wants Aubrey to know that she has just entered the Sane family inferno. She wants Aubrey to feel the heat and either measure up or back down. "Well, hello there, Aubrey. Good to see you again," Kennedy delivers with purposeful insincerity.

Aubrey swallows back the urge to walk out of the door. Instead, she simply returns Kennedy's disingenuous smile, letting Kennedy know that she can't intimidate her. "Good to see you again as well."

Aubrey looks at Daniel, trying to read his demeanor. He won't make eye contact with her.

"Right this way, dear. I hope you like chicken piccata." Sylvia takes Aubrey's hand and leads her to the dining room. They sit at a large wooden table beautifully set with cloth napkins, authentic silverware, and wine glasses of sparkling juice and water. Daniel, Delmain, Sylvia, and Aubrey sit while Kennedy serves the food. Once everyone has a plate, they bow their heads and listen as Daniel blesses the food.

Everyone starts eating. Only the sound of silverware scraping against glass plates fills the room.

Aubrey looks around the table at their faces, ready for the fire to rain down. With every second that passes, she grows weary of wondering why things seem strained and awkward. When Aubrey makes eye contact with Sylvia, she smiles sweetly as if everything is butterflies and rainbows. Next, she looks to Daniel for answers. He wiggles his brows, attempting to put her at ease. Disappointed in Daniel, she rolls her eyes as she looks away, storing up a pocket full of contempt to release on him later. When her gaze lands on Kennedy, she gives Aubrey a stale glare wanting her to feel uncomfortable. Lastly, Aubrey makes eye contact with Delmain. He drops his fork and huffs out a resolved breath. He isn't the type of man to tinker or tiptoe around feelings, and Aubrey is grateful for it.

"Aubrey," Delmain calls her name, breaking the silence. "Daniel tells me that he entrusted you with private information."

"Honey," Sylvia warns her husband as if he is embarrassing her.

Daniel stiffly shakes his head from side to side, cautioning his dad. His eyes are intense with confusion. Why? Daniel thinks. Why can't his dad honor his way of handling business? Daniel gives his head one more hard shake, pleading with his dad to respect his wishes. Delmain ignores them both. "In this family, we put everything on the table. Therefore, I must put out that the only people who know about Daniel's bouts of stupidity are the people in this room, so if that information gets out…"

Aubrey releases a breath that she didn't realize she had been holding, happy to finally know what the fuss is about. "I would never leak his personal information."

"We know that," Sylvia says, giving her husband another warning look.

Delmain does not heed her warning. "I'm not giving the media a chance to use my son's face to portray him as a problem in society."

"I wholeheartedly agree," Aubrey assures him.

"What if you two break up? Are we going to have to pay you to keep the information private?"

"Dad!" Daniel's voice booms throughout the house. "That is enough."

"I'm not interested in your family's money," Aubrey speaks matter-of-factly, a bit perturbed by knowing what his family truly thinks of her.

"Are you sure about that?" Kennedy jumps in to question. "Because you wanted nothing to do with Daniel a few months ago. Now he's calling you family."

Daniel slams his fist on the table. "I said enough!"

"We're just asking questions," Kennedy defends. "If she's going to be family, she must know how to roll with the punches."

Sylvia stands up in her chair, taking control of the situation. Each member of her family is too unrelenting to allow them to have at each other. "Enough!" She speaks, and everyone listens. She looks toward Aubrey, sitting tall with her shoulders back, feeling respect for her. Still, she doesn't respect her enough to think she's suitable for her son. "Aubrey, will you please join me outside."

Throwing her cloth napkin on the table, Aubrey stands and follows Sylvia onto the front porch. She hears Daniel erupt into a yell the moment they step foot outside.

Aubrey and Sylvia sit next to each other in lawn chairs. Sylvia takes Aubrey's hand in hers, gently stroking it. "Please excuse my husband and daughter. They can be a bit abrasive, but they mean well."

Not in the mood for excuses, Aubrey doesn't pretend she is okay with Kennedy and Delmain's behavior. On the contrary, their attitude toward her is monstrous. They spoke to her as if their money made them superior. Like they are gods, and she is a dog.

"I want to be straightforward with you," Sylvia continues, the sweetness leaving her tone. "Daniel is particularly vulnerable right now, and we must protect him. Deep down, Daniel is still finding his way. He's clinging to whatever you two have going on so he can get through. I just hope you're aware that this is a phase. If you care for him at all, you will end it so he can pursue his football career with a clear mind."

Aubrey snatches her hand away from Sylvia and storms off the porch. Daniel walks outside just in time to see Aubrey open his car door and push the start button. As she pulls away, he runs off the porch to jump in the car.

"How can people so crazy be named Sane?" Aubrey yells.

"You're right. My family is trippin', but they'll get used to you being in my life."

Aubrey slams the brakes, bringing the car to a halting stop. Daniel braces himself against the dashboard to avoid flying through the windshield. "You expect me to put up with that?" she yells again.

"Let's not yell at each other, Bree," Daniel states calmly.

Aubrey takes a few calming breaths. "This is why I was happy being friends. There was no pressure and no expectations."

"Friends?" Daniel says, his eyes wide with worry. "I'm not going back to that!"

"It feels like we're trying to force things to happen."

"Who's forcing? I want you, and you want me, right?"

"Yes, we want each other, but are we following our hearts or leading them?"

"We're leading them toward each other."

Aubrey turns her head to look out of the window, unsure.

"Look at me, Bree Bree," Daniel pleads.

Aubrey continues looking out of the window. Daniel takes hold of her chin, turning her face toward him so that he can look into her eyes. "Talk to me," he says.

Aubrey looks at him for a long moment, not knowing what to say. The longer she looks, the more she melts. She can't take seeing the hurt in his eyes. Finally, she reaches out to smooth the worry in his brows. "Stop looking at me like that."

Her tender smile grants him peace. "I apologize for my family," he says genuinely. "They still see me as the foolish boy who almost ruined everything. But they're still learning to trust the man I've become."

Aubrey simply nods, accepting his apology while also noting the day as a cautionary sign.

AUBREY SITS STILL under the moonlight, deeply into her morning routine. A rhythmic knock on her door breaks her focus. Recognizing the pattern of his knock, she opens the door for Daniel. He is wearing a button-up shirt and black slacks. His clothes always fit perfectly over every muscle of his body as if he has them custom made for him. "You look very handsome," Aubrey compliments. "Where are you going?"

"On a date with you," he replies smoothly.

"It's six in the morning."

"Go get dressed," he urges.

He is beaming with delight; she can't disappoint such a face. Without another word, Aubrey complies. She hurries into her bathroom, cleans herself up, and resurfaces minutes later. She stands before him in a simple white dress that perfectly flatters her curves and skin tone. Biting his lip, Daniel steps back and admires her. His eyes linger on her shamelessly. "Mm," he moans, his eyes fluttering. "As always, you look like a goddess, but there is something about seeing you in a white dress..."

Aubrey smiles. "You're always flirting."

"I'm not trying to flatter you. I'm very serious."

The tenacity etched into his expression takes Aubrey's breath away, sending flutters through her. She struggles to come up with a response.

He flashes his signature full smile, loving how he leaves her speechless. "Come on," he says, taking hold of her hand and leading her toward the exit.

They drive for forty-five minutes before arriving at a mansion guarded by a large gate. Daniel rolls down his window to talk into an intercom. "Reservation for Daniel Sane."

The gates open, and Daniel drives through. Wide-eyed, Aubrey looks out the window, taking in the scenic path and all its splendor. "This is it," Daniel tells her excitedly.

Dipping her head to look up through the windshield, Aubrey takes in the tall archways full of red-and-pink roses leading down a pathway to a large greenhouse. They get out of the car and follow the path while holding hands. Daniel looks over at her every few steps with pride oozing from within. He playfully squeezes her hand before bringing it to his lips to caress her soft skin, not missing a moment to dote over her as they continue down the path. Once inside the greenhouse, butterflies greet them, fluttering around their heads. Lavender plants provide a romantic aroma pleasing to their noses. Aubrey stops to appreciate the lavender and breathes it in. They can't see the birds, but their morning praise supplies a musical ambiance. Outside the greenhouse walls, deer prance around, nibbling on greenery that the owners strategically planted to invite them in.

"Whoa," Aubrey breathes.

"It's even better than the pictures," Daniel adds with just as much exhilaration.

In the middle of thriving green plants and colorful flowers is a small wooden table with two hammock chairs on either side. A platter of fresh fruit sits on the table next to a teapot. They settle into the hammocks, swinging back and forth while eating the fruit. "This is beautiful," Aubrey marvels while biting into a perfectly round purple grape. She moans as the sweet juice pleases her palate.

Daniel admires her flawless beauty as she closes her eyes and lifts her face toward the morning sun. As he had hoped, the place enamors her. Step one of his plan is a success. He begins working on the next phase of his plan. "Imagine sitting outside every morning like this, drinking your tea and doing your morning routine," Daniel offers while pouring a cup of tea and handing it to her. He needs to show her a possible future with him since she can't seem to see anything but reuniting with her mom in her future.

"That would be amazing," she replies, sipping on the tea.

"I can imagine you with your mat and journal, stretching in the sun and writing whatever flows from within while drinking from a nearby stream," he continues painting the picture for her.

Aubrey's eyes quiver to a close, allowing his words to lull her.

Daniel gives her a moment to visualize herself waking up daily in the beautiful scenery. "Would you like that?" Daniel asks.

"I would love that."

"Whatever house we settle into after the draft, we'll ensure it has space for a big greenhouse."

His solemn tone of voice pulls Aubrey away from her happy place. She opens her eyes and meets his penetrating stare. She can't pinpoint why, but an unsettling feeling deepens in her gut. She picks up another grape to avoid his eyes.

"We're just dreaming," he says, noticing her shift.

"You think the Cleveland Browns will pick you?" Aubrey mentions the NFL team closest to their Ohio home.

Daniel shakes his head slowly and steadily. "Based on my research, the Texans need a wide receiver. So it's a strong possibility that I could end up in Houston."

Aubrey's face twitches, unable to mask her panic. "If you played for Cleveland, at least we would be close to each other," she tries again.

Daniel sits quietly, patiently bearing with her. "We'll be close to each other no matter what because you're coming with me, right?"

The unsettling feeling grows more intense. "We've never discussed it," Aubrey says, stalling. Of course, she wants to be where he is, but the thought of moving far away without settling things with her mom makes her feel incomplete.

"That's why we're discussing it now. The combine is soon. The possibility of me leaving within the next week to start training is very likely. Are you coming with me, or are we spending months apart?"

Aubrey takes another sip of tea and tries to ignore the empty feeling nagging her. "We'll have time to figure it out. We don't have to rush."

"Aubrey, Grant wants me to start training immediately in Texas."

"Okay. We can still figure it out," Aubrey says simply.

"Why does it feel like you're avoiding my question?"

"Why does it feel like I'm in the middle of a business meeting?"

"Because we are," Daniel answers truthfully. "You and I are a business, and we need a plan that goes beyond the current moment."

Aubrey sits back in her seat, having conflicting feelings. A part of her feels excited about a future with him, while a different part feels smothered.

"What's happening right now?" Daniel probes when she doesn't tell him what he desires. "Are you feeling like you don't want to come?"

"I don't know what I'm feeling. I just want to think about it."

"Think about what?" he says, his nostrils flaring out. "I want to make it clear, if I haven't before, I want you in my future forever. As my best friend. As my life partner. As my wife. As the mother to my children. I don't want to live one day without you."

"I don't want one second without you," she admits honestly. "I have every intention to be in your future."

Her words put him at ease. He imagines her lounging across their king-sized bed in a cozy pair of pajamas, her hair spread across a silk pillowcase, and a ring on her finger. "Alright," he says softly. "Just making sure we're moving in the same direction."

Aubrey stuffs the feelings tugging on her insides, chalking it up as nerves. She knows without a doubt that Daniel has a place in her life. He has been consistently patient with her, kind, and gentle. They align spiritually. He is her dearest friend, and she can talk to him about anything. "We're clearly moving in that same direction," she assures him and herself.

Daniel studies her expression, trying to find a hint of doubt, but he can see that she means what she said. He briefly wonders about her hesitancy but decides not to read too much into it. He realizes it must be difficult for her to leave everything she knows to move to an unfamiliar place. It is his job and pleasure to make her feel comfortable, covered, and stable. "You're not going to have to worry about a thing," he guarantees.

"I know," she replies with an easy smile.

Chapter Fifteen

DANIEL AND TRAVIS WATCH Aubrey from a distance. She sits with her legs crossed at the top of the bleachers and her nose in a book. Travis turns on his camera phone and presses the record button.

"Go get her, Bro," Travis encourages.

Daniel jogs to the top of the bleachers and sits next to Aubrey. The grin stretched across his face is contagious. Looking up from her book, Aubrey glances at him, and his smile spreads to her face. "Hey, handsome," she says, acknowledging his presence.

"Hey beautiful," Daniel responds, the smile carrying over to his eyes.

"Why are you smiling so hard?" she questions.

"Because I think about you all day and get so excited when I finally see you."

His words sweep Aubrey into a dizzying fairytale. "You're the sweetest," she utters, twinkles visible in her eyes.

The same twinkles sparkle in his eyes as he gazes back at Aubrey. "I want to marry you, Bree Bree."

He isn't down on one knee or anything, so Aubrey misses his resolve. "I can see us married in a few years."

"What do you think about becoming Mrs. Sane before the draft?"

The spark burns out of her gaze, turning her warm brown eyes into black ice. "The draft is like two months away."

"Mm hmm," he confirms.

"You want to get married within the next couple of months?" She barely chokes out the sentence.

Daniel shoves his hand into his pocket and pulls out a ring box. He opens it, revealing a halo of glistening diamonds.

Aubrey covers her mouth, not in excitement but to conceal the panic wreaking havoc inside her. "Daniel," she speaks his name through a shallow breath. "I already agreed to marry you and move wherever you're drafted at some point—"

Daniel puts up his hand, interrupting her statement. "At some point?"

"Yes. I never said within the next couple of months. I'm still trying to figure things out with my mom," Aubrey explains.

Daniel rubs his hand over his face, releasing a long shallow breath. "Bree Bree," he says her name as if he is working hard to be patient. "Your mom only lives two hours away, yet you haven't gotten in your car and driven to see her. I need you to make that drive, handle your business, and then come back to me so we can continue our life together."

Aubrey reaches out to close the ring box and pushes it back toward him. "Don't do that to me. Don't rush me just because you don't want your life to be inconvenienced."

Daniel looks down at the ring box against his chest. His plans and his face crumble simultaneously. He struggles to understand how she couldn't feel what he feels for her. Since he first saw her, he knew his forever was with her. He has never been surer about a decision in his life. "So, you're saying no?" he asks for clarity.

"I'm saying yes, but not in two months. I need a few years."

"I'm not waiting years to marry you, Aubrey."

"And I'm not marrying you in two months. I need you to wait for me."

Daniel repeatedly blinks, trying to imagine himself waiting years for her. He can't imagine it. Thinking of life without her accessible to him is too unbearable. Without another word, he stands and starts down the bleachers. He notices Travis still recording at the bottom and shifts his weight to go in another direction. His brain moves faster than his feet, and he stumbles down the bleachers before he can catch himself.

A deep bellow of agony fills the arena. Travis and Coach run to his aid. Aubrey watches the horror play out with round eyes, unable to bring herself to move. Coach and Travis help Daniel to his feet. He attempts to step down the bleachers, but his leg buckles underneath him. Coach and Travis hold him firmly, not letting him fall again. Finally, they help him limp into the training room.

Aubrey remains on the bleachers, unmoving and in a daze. She is silently praying that he isn't seriously injured. When she finishes praying, she tells herself to stand and check on him. Her legs won't listen. A part of her doesn't want to go check on him because she can't bear to see him in pain, especially the pain she has caused. Aubrey looks like a statue as she sits, doing nothing with herself, staring at the track. Eventually, Coach reappears and taps Aubrey on the shoulder. "Come on. We're not having practice today."

"Is it bad?" Aubrey asks, wincing as she awaits the answer.

"It's not too bad. Daniel pulled his hamstring. He will be fine."

Aubrey clutches her collar for strength, hating that he must deal with a pulled muscle so close to the draft. "Can I go see him?"

"No. Not a good idea," Coach advises firmly.

Something about the assurance in Coach's voice intrigues Aubrey. She needs to know why Coach is so sure that she shouldn't go see him. Defiant and determined, Aubrey shoots to her feet, moves quickly down the bleachers, and enters the training room. Sylvia, Delmain, and Kennedy shock her when she walks in; she hadn't noticed them enter the arena. She wondered how long she had been in a daze on the bleachers. Daniel's family stands over him, stroking his shoulders with compassion. Daniel's arms are crossed over his face, covering his emotion. The trainer has his leg in an ice pack bubble sleeve that extends the entire length of his leg.

"Now you can move on with a clear head," Sylvia says softly.

Aubrey takes another step inside, alerting everyone of her presence. Kennedy rolls her eyes indignantly. "Why are you here?"

Daniel pulls his arm away from his face, revealing red eyes and his merciless fury. "Get out!" he warns through clenched teeth.

147

The ice in his voice causes Aubrey to flinch back. She expected him to be upset but thought they could discuss their differences. "I couldn't leave without checking on you," she says timidly.

The muscle in his jaw tightened. "Let's make it simple and be completely done with each other," Daniel clarifies. His harsh tone and cold stare don't match the kindhearted man who brings her so much comfort. She isn't ready to accept this angry version of him. She knows her Daniel is there if she can just get beyond the resentment.

"You don't mean that," she says softly. "This doesn't have to be an all-or-nothing situation?"

"Aubrey, get out," he repeats coldly.

"No," she refuses. "We're not done. I love you, and I will marry you. I just need some time." She tells him how things are going to go.

Daniel glares at her, his eyes void of the love they once shared. Only his disdain for her is evident. He turns to his mom. "Can you please get her out of here?" He put his arms back over his face, blocking the rest out.

"Daniel," Aubrey speaks his name, refusing to be ignored.

Daniel doesn't respond. She repeats his name. Still, no response. She may as well be talking to a stone wall. Finally, Sylvia steps in between them, blocking her view of Daniel. Sylvia does not say any words. Everything she needs to say is imprinted in her solemn expression, conveying her seriousness. Aubrey has enough sense to know when to tap out. With a frustrated huff, she turns and leaves the room.

OVER THE NEXT WEEK, Daniel constantly declines Aubrey's calls. Every time his phone rings, her photo appears on his screen. He remembers when he took the photo. Aubrey was sitting on the edge of his sofa. The sun was setting and beaming through the window, glorifying her. She wore a white shirt that fell off her shoulder, showing off her radiant unblemished, caramel-colored skin. They were supposed to be watching a movie together, but instead, they were watching each other. His gaze traveled from her exposed shoulder to her defined collarbone, neck, and face. He studied the structure of her full lips, lively eyes, ethnic nose, sculpted chin, and curved eyebrows. "You are freaking stunning," he breathed. "You look like someone painted you." Aubrey smiled so beautifully that he felt a nudge in his abdomen, weakening him. He grabbed his phone, needing to capture what his eyes were seeing. "Don't move," he instructed. Aubrey submitted, staying in place so he could photograph her. He saved the photo to the home screen on his phone.

Growing tired of seeing her exquisite face, he deletes her photo and number from his phone. Calling him repeatedly is her last avenue to get through to him. He had moved into his sister's house to avoid running into her in the hallway. He also decided to stop going into the arena, mainly to avoid her. He needed to focus on healing his leg so he could be ready to perform at the combine. He secures his decision by blocking her number so she can't get through to him. "I'm done with her," he mumbles to himself. When he thinks about leaving Ohio without her, agony pounces on his chest. He knows that once he is gone, the breakup will be real. There won't be a chance to accidentally run into her in the student union or the elevator. Once he leaves the state, he leaves Aubrey, and something about that doesn't sit right with him.

"Get up," Delmain demands, interrupting Daniel's thoughts.

Daniel looks up at him, perplexed. He is resting on the couch with an ice pack under his hamstring. "What's up, Dad?"

"You've been sitting on this couch in the same spot for a week. You pulled a muscle; you didn't break a leg. You can get up and move around."

Daniel sighs, wanting his dad to leave him alone with his thoughts. "Dad, I'm aware that my leg isn't broken."

"But your heart is, huh?"

There is a compassion in Delmain's voice that causes Daniel to tear up. His dad grew up in South Africa on tough love and diligent work. He has a low tolerance for anything that isn't education, cultivating oneself, and currency. Anytime he entertains anything outside those categories, Daniel knows it comes from a place of pure love. Unable to speak, Daniel simply nods his head.

Delmain puts his hand on Daniel's shoulder and squeezes it. "Come on, let's go grab some breakfast."

Daniel and Delmain sit across from each other in a booth. They have a spread of food in front of them as if they ordered everything on the menu. "You're walking well," Delmain comments while slicing his pancakes. "How's it feeling?"

Daniel stretches out his leg, testing the muscle. "It's a little sore, but it's going to get me through that combine."

"That's right. I love to hear it." Delmain points to the fruit and oatmeal on the table. "And I see you're sticking to your eating plan. I'm proud of you," his dad praises while putting a bite of pancakes dripping in syrup in his mouth.

Daniel chuckles while pulling the fruit toward him, but he doesn't pick up a fork. He isn't in the mood to eat. Delmain takes one last bite of his pancakes and pushes the plate aside, leaning his elbows on the table. "So, tell me how you're feeling, son?" He gives Daniel full permission to be in his feelings while he patiently listens.

Running his hand over his face, Daniel breathes a long sigh before beginning. "Okay, so, Aubrey." He sighs again as a result of speaking her name. She exhausted him. Yet, he still can't get enough of her. "She was one of the first people I met when I arrived on campus. That moment I first saw her is still embedded in my memory. It wasn't normal, Dad. I thought she was perfection physically, but the attraction was much stronger than physical. I can't quite explain it other than a love-at-first-sight type of thing or a soulmate. Innately, I knew she was supposed to be part of my life. I remember watching her run down the track. Her talent left me in awe. The moment she finished the race, reality shifted into a daydream. I'm not exaggerating when I say that I saw an entire future with her playout in my vision—marriage, babies, TV appearances, us standing in front of crowds of people together. Initially, I rejected the vision because I came here to change my life, not meet a girl, right?"

Delmain nods exaggeratedly in agreement.

"Dad, that girl was everywhere. I couldn't get away from her if I tried. She was my neighbor, my teammate, and my groupmate. It felt like all creation was slapping me upside my head, saying, pay attention to her. We became great friends, and our connection felt magical. After a while, the visions became more elaborate. When I envisioned myself playing in the NFL, she was in the stands wearing my jersey. She picked out the furniture when I saw myself moving into my first home." Daniel drops his head in his hands and squeezes his face as if trying to push out the stress. "I just don't understand why creation would force us together just for life to lead us in different directions?" Daniel complains.

"Is that why you asked her to marry you? So, she would move with you?" his dad asks.

Daniel nods, embarrassed by how his desperate attempt to keep her failed.

"Let me tell you a story about your mom and me. Sylvia … that's my girl. Our vibe has always been on the same wavelength. When we met, building my career absorbed me. And just like you, I asked her to sacrifice to be with me. All my requests were met by her. In exchange, I made sure she didn't want for anything. I gave her everything I had emotionally, mentally, and spiritually and never wavered. But when she got sick, there was nothing I could give or provide to make her better. Your mom went through a season where she had to rediscover herself and remember the power she possessed within. And I had to let her go, so I didn't become her crutch. She had to decide what life was going to be for herself. Once she found her way, she returned to me as a dynamic woman, even more beautiful than the person I thought I was in love with. I had to rise up to meet her where she ascended to."

"So, you're suggesting that I let her go?" Daniel huffs.

Delmain patiently smiles despite Daniel's attitude. "I want you to understand how time works. When people don't get what they desire within a certain timeframe, they think they missed out. However, time happens in cycles. Everything that happened once will come around again, just like the seasons. So you must be in the proper position when the time comes to seize the opportunity."

"What are you saying, Dad?" Daniel urges him to make his point.

If you had visions of Aubrey in your future, it doesn't mean it won't happen just because it's not happening right now. That vision could be for a different season. When married people are having trouble in paradise, the advice they get is to take time and do all they can before settling on a divorce. So why not give that same advice before getting married? People get married as fast as they can get a piece of chicken in the drive-thru. What's the rush? If this girl is truly your soulmate, then you have forever."

Daniel tilts his head to one side, pondering his dad's wisdom. "Even if we end up on different ends of the country?"

"Doesn't matter where you are. Just like you found each other the first time, it can easily happen again. Trust the process. Aubrey has to find her power within the same way you had to find yours. She's still healing from her childhood and finding her way. Allow her to do that."

Daniel sighs, taking another moment to mull over Delmain's words. Closing his eyes, he releases another sigh, knowing that his dad is right. He wants nothing more than to pack Aubrey up and carry her to wherever life leads him. But that would have to wait for a different season, which is both comforting and heartbreaking.

Chapter Sixteen

IT HAS BEEN an entire month since Aubrey last saw or heard from Daniel. He does not answer her phone calls or attend the mental success group in person. She knocks on his door every night, but still, he does not answer. After four weeks of silence, she goes from sad to extremely angry. She hates that he ended things without giving her a chance to reconcile. At first, she remained hopeful that he would come around, but his consistent absence overwhelmed her. She misses hearing the deep rumble in his voice whenever he speaks her name. She misses rubbing his head while he rests on her chest for a midday nap. She misses the sweet kisses he places over her neck whenever he desires. She longs for the comforting warmth she feels when their skin touches and how his scent lulls her into a dream. Needing to see and hear him, she picks up her phone and opens social media. She types his name into the search bar, preparing to watch his videos and view his photos. After typing in his name, the search ends with zero results. He has blocked her from his social media page.

Not being able to access him makes Aubrey feel powerless. Her once numb heart begins to regain its feeling, and she intensely feels every yank as Daniel's abandonment extracts her heart from her chest. Sitting on her futon, she stares at the photo collage on her wall. She keeps looking at the word family. The longer she looks, the angrier she becomes. Why does family keep abandoning her? Is it so hard to talk things through, she thinks. She jumps from the futon, snatches the collage from the wall, and drops it on the floor, causing the glass to shatter. Breaking the frame doesn't give her the satisfaction she hoped it would. Instead, it only makes her think of Daniel more. Aubrey picks up one of the four-by-six photos from the floor, examining it. In the photo, Daniel and Aubrey pretend to bite an enormous lollipop.

Daniel had taken the photo at the skating arcade. The memory of that day is something she treasures. Daniel had such piercing tenderness in his eyes. She knew then that he loved her differently than she had ever experienced. Aubrey picks up the other photos from the floor, imagining how Daniel thoughtfully chose each picture and then sent them through a one-hour printing service. She imagines him carefully putting each image into the frame—a gesture of love meant to uplift her after a heartbreaking day. Her eyes begin to moisten. If he loved her then, how could he not love her now? Aubrey stands rigid while deep in thought for a long moment. Every beautiful memory of them together plays like a film in her thoughts. When the film concludes, the absence of love leaves her feeling hollow within. Needing to rescue herself from reminiscing, she grabs her phone and follows her heart instead of leading it. Jace's name is on her screen, and the phone is ringing. No matter her inconsistency, Jace persistently pursued her. She appreciates Jace for not discarding her.

"You called!" Jace celebrated in a loud tone.

Aubrey giggles, trying her best to sound cheerful. "How are you?"

"I'm still trying to catch up with you. Have you eaten dinner yet? If not, can I take you out?" he offers.

An apprehensive sensation rumbles in her gut as she cringes at how easy it is to get what she wants from Jace. Surely, he expects reciprocity. Aubrey closes her eyes for a second. When she reopens them, she wears the same desolate expression as the day her mom didn't attend her track meet. The avatar is back. Self-preserving Aubrey is the only version of herself who can survive this abandonment. She can't allow herself to care about anything. What is the point of caring just to end up with the same broken heart every time? "Yes," she answers tonelessly. "I'll go to dinner," she clarifies pointedly.

JACE PICKS HER UP in his old-school Charger. Vulgar rap music blasts in her ears. On any other occasion, she would reach out to turn off the music and start a debate about the sexual objectification of women. But she convinces herself that she doesn't care about anything anymore. She listens to the insults thrown over the rhythmic beat bobbing her head. As they drive down the street, Jace keeps looking at her, noticing her zoned-out demeanor.

"You ever ate here before?" he asks, pulling into the parking lot of Sloppy Burger.

Aubrey looks up at the sign and rolls her eyes. She remembers explicitly telling him that she does not eat Sloppy Burger. She has told him several times. Apparently, he doesn't listen to her. But, again, she doesn't care. "Let's see what it's talking about," she replies.

They enter the restaurant and encounter a long line. "This place is always poppin' because it's so good," Jace says as they settle into the line, the drool practically running from his mouth. Crossing her arms, Aubrey quietly occupies herself, checking out the restaurant. She reads over the autographed jerseys framed on the wall beside signed photos of famous athletes and coaches. She follows Jace's gaze to the flat-screen televisions bolted at each booth, programmed to the local sports station. It isn't the typical place to take a girl for a date.

"What can I get for you tonight?" a young man working the register asks Jace once they are at the front of the line.

"Let me get that, barbecue cheddar burger," Jace orders while looking at the menu. "And a large chocolate shake."

"Anything else?" he asks.

Jace looks at Aubrey. She shakes her head. "You don't want anything?" Jace probes, confused. Aubrey shakes her head again. "Add a small fry and pineapple mango smoothie."

For a brief moment, he can see the life resurface in Aubrey's expression. Jace remembering her favorite drink impresses her. One corner of her mouth pulls up into a half smile before she retreats behind her wall again.

The cashier punches in the order. "Fourteen dollars, even."

Jace hands the cashier fourteen dollars exactly. In return, the cashier gives Jace a table number, instructing them to sit anywhere until someone delivers the food to the table.

Jace and Aubrey slide into a booth in the back of the restaurant. Jace hangs his arm over the back of the booth, kicks up his leg, and starts watching sports. He doesn't attempt to start a conversation. Instead, he just stares at the TV.

Aubrey sits across from him, eyeing him suspiciously. Jace isn't the quiet type. He can turn any topic into an exciting conversation. He is up to something.

"Oh, look." Jace points at the television screen. "They're talking about your boy."

Aubrey follows his line of sight to the screen. The sports commentators display Daniel's photo while they discuss the upcoming draft.

"It's looking like your boy might be a first-round pick. He may end up back in Texas. Are you going with him?"

Jace questions with malice, alerting Aubrey why he agreed to their meeting so quickly. He had an agenda. "Why are you asking me about him?"

"Oh, right! He broke up with you. I did hear all the rumors. It's why you called me, right? Your misery desired my company?" Jace delivers the insult with perfect disdain like he had been rehearsing it all night. Yes, this meeting is about payback, indeed.

Aubrey crosses her arms. "So, you brought me here to get at me?"

"I brought you here because I wanted you to know what it feels like to have someone use you and throw you away."

"What are you talking about?" she asks.

"You remember the last real conversation we had?" He brings up a conversation they had over a year ago. Jace had invited her out to lunch. He picked her up and drove her to a nearby park where he had set up a lovely picnic. A picnic in the park was on her list of dream dates, and he had made it come true. He was thoughtful in preparing her favorite foods and drinks. The meal was spread over a vibrant yellow blanket. His gesture was lovely but left a sour taste in Aubrey's mouth. Aubrey had decided that Jace would be a better friend than mate, though she adored him. Whenever they were together, she never stopped laughing. He understood her in a way that made her existence germane to creation. Jace was wonderful. Her one complaint against him was that he was too sensual. He treated love and sex like they were synonymous. "I told you how much I care about you. And then the next day, I tried calling but couldn't reach you." Aubrey sucks in her upper lip, ashamed of her behavior. She had abandoned him the same way Daniel had left her. She is reaping what she has sown. "In fact, I couldn't reach you until I happened to run into you that day on campus. You promised that we'd talk, but still nothing. And then you agreed to go to the fashion show with me. You even ran up and hugged me like I was your favorite person, but that was just to make your boyfriend jealous, wasn't it?"

Aubrey blinks rapidly, unable to deny her shortcomings. She guiltily fidgets with a fork on the table, thinking of something to tell him. Eventually, she settles on the truth. "You're right," Aubrey admits. "I was mad at Daniel, so I agreed to go to the fashion show with you. I owe you an apology because that was wrong. Also, I should have talked to you instead of ghosting you."

"I want to know why you ended things?" Jace questions, ready to get answers from her.

"Because you wanted more than friendship, but we didn't vibe like that."

Jace laughs haughtily. "You are lying to yourself!" Jace accuses, refusing to accept her response. "I've never vibed with anyone as well as we do," he says in exasperation.

"We're good at being friends, but that doesn't mean we're supposed to tie our souls together."

Jace rolls his eyes. "Tie our souls together?" he repeats, imitating her. "Why you gotta make everything deep. We're young! We're grown. We are amazing together. Why not enjoy it?"

"See, what I mean?" Aubrey throws out. "You're more focused on getting your rocks off."

The corners of Jace's mouth flinch, but he straightens up his face, refusing to laugh. After a second, he explodes with laughter, unable to remain angry. "Get my rocks off?" he teases. He permits himself to laugh for a moment before getting back to business. "I'm only laughing because that's funny, but I'm still mad. I know I'm a sexy man who can get a lot of women, but that doesn't mean I don't have feelings."

Aubrey smiles at the way he compliments himself.

"I'm serious," Jace continues. "You do this thing where you only consider how you feel. You don't look at the situation in its entirety or consider what the other people involved are going through."

Aubrey's eyes grow wide and round. She stares past Jace, instantly having an epiphany. She goes deep in thought, considering his words. She considers what it must be like for Daniel to move wherever the league desires to pursue his dreams. She thinks of her mother and what it must have cost her to push her only child out of the house to protect her. It is the first time she thinks beyond her feelings. "You're not wrong, Jace," Aubrey breathes. "You're not wrong. And I sincerely apologize."

Jace reaches his hand across the table, offering his forgiveness. Aubrey places her hand in his. Enclosing her hand, Jace pulls Aubrey to her feet and wraps her in his arms. "You're still one of my favorite people, and I don't want to throw that away. I need your friendship always. Is that cool with you?" he requests.

"It's cool with me."

"Well, cool," Jace chuckles. "Let's get out of here and get some real food."

"I knew you remembered that I didn't like this place." Aubrey playfully punches him in the arm while Jace laughs freely.

Later that night, when Aubrey arrives home, she methodically executes her evening routine, still thinking of Jace's words. As she climbs under the covers and pulls them over her face, she carefully thinks about what is on her mind. Typically, Aubrey commands every thought to keep herself from drowning in grief, but she decides to allow her mind to be free for the moment. Tossing and turning as the rails creak under the mattress, she lies aware of her thoughts without judging, defending, or responding. Instead, she simply lets her inward voice speak while listening intently. It is morning when she realizes that sleep has completely evaded her. She knows that she has something important to do.

Getting out of bed, she showers, dresses for the day, and goes to her car. She feels a sense of peace as she starts the engine and begins the journey. She travels the familiar roads from Ohio to Pennsylvania as if she has done it a thousand times. The trip takes her through valleys and narrow streets twisting at the base of large mountains covered with trees. She journeys past wide rivers glistening in the morning sun. She rides through small towns losing cellphone service and sight of anything enticing besides a general store. The two-hour drive feels like it takes five minutes when she finally reaches her desired destination. Aubrey parks down the street from her childhood home and watches the house. It isn't long before the garage door opens, and the Benz pulls out, speeding through the suburban neighborhood. Five minutes later, like clockwork, her mother appears in the front yard to tend to what Aubrey thinks is an already perfectly put-together flower bed. She takes a minute to observe her mom, watching her sweep little pieces of escaped mulch back into the flower bed. Her mom examines each plant like a doctor checking a patient's health.

Filling her cheeks with air, Aubrey releases a long breath from a small opening in her lips. Not letting herself think about anything other than accomplishing her goal, Aubrey takes hold of the door handle and pushes it open. She feels her heartbeat increase from a normal rhythm to a raging pulse, but she keeps putting one foot in front of the other. When Aubrey reaches the beginning of the driveway, her mom looks up and sees her approaching. Nia squints her eyes even though she has perfect vision, ensuring she is seeing correctly. Nia stands still in shock as she watches her baby girl approach. Aubrey inspects Nia's eyes as she observes her walking up. She waits for her mom to give her the smile that stops her whole world, but she does not. Instead, Nia takes a moment to look down at the ground as if Aubrey's presence disappoints her before looking back up to greet her.

"Aubrey? Aubrey! Aubrey. Aubrey..." She calls her name four times as if she doesn't know what else to say.

Aubrey responds with a small smile. Tipping her head slightly to one side, Aubrey stands just feet away from her mom, studying her features and body language to see what is different. Five years have brought little change. She still wears her hair in the same pulled-back ponytail hairstyle. She is still wearing the same style of black leggings with an oversized black t-shirt. The only thing different about her is the missing smile. She seems inherently sad. Opening her arms, Aubrey steps toward her mom, and they embrace. Nia squeezes her tightly, holding on to her for the longest time. Eventually, they release each other, but Nia goes in for more, kissing all over Aubrey's cheeks like she did when Aubrey was a kid.

"Look at how beautiful you are," Nia compliments, giving her a once-over.

Aubrey can feel sadness emitting from her mom even though Nia is trying to appear happy. Aubrey's objective for making the two-hour drive changes from wanting her perspective to wanting to see her smile genuinely. "Thank you," she replies to her mom sweetly. "Do you need any help?" Aubrey points to the immaculate flower bed.

"Sure." Nia grabs her watering can and plant food and passes it to Aubrey. She instructs Aubrey to fill the watering can with water at the hose and add a scoop of plant food. Aubrey follows her instructions, assisting her while she goes to work in the dirt. "Can't believe you're here," Nia marvels aloud.

"I know, right," Aubrey answers coolly.

They keep up a casual conversation while meticulously perfecting the flower bed. Aubrey tells her about college, the mentorship group, and the crazy situations Lily seemed to get her in. Nia listens and asks follow-up questions that keep the conversation moving as they relocate to different spots in the flower garden, pulling the tiniest weeds and collecting twigs. As the day progresses, Aubrey realizes she must leave soon. She moves the conversation in a purposeful direction.

"Track has been great too," Aubrey commences the necessary dialogue.

Nia winces, discerning that it is time to have a difficult conversation. "Right. How did that last meet go?"

"It wasn't the best," Aubrey answers honestly. "Why didn't you come?"

Nia's hands stop rummaging through the dirt, and she looks away from Aubrey, staring at nothing. After a long pause and no reply, Aubrey walks around to force her mom to look her in the face.

"I didn't come here to attack you. I came to understand. To see things from your perspective." Aubrey tells her.

"What do you want to understand?"

"Why was it me you got rid of and not him?"

Nia sighs, communicating that she doesn't want to have the conversation even though she is willing. "You're not going to understand my relationship. It dates back to when you were just a baby. Just know he was here for us when no one else was, and I want to do the same for him as he goes through."

"Goes through what?"

Nia starts shaking her head before Aubrey can finish her sentence. But then, Aubrey remembers she isn't there to convince her mom to leave her man or change her mind about her life choices. That is God's job, not hers, so she lets it go. Aubrey must be okay with pieces of the story, knowing her mom isn't the type to find solace in transparency. Nia'a solitude comes from not giving people the privilege of knowing everything about her. "Okay, well, can you help me understand why you never called me again?"

Nia wraps her arms around herself, uncomfortable because she is losing control of her emotions. Unauthorized tears fill her eyes. She turns away from Aubrey to hide them as they drip onto her cheeks. "Because I can't stand to see how you are now," she croaks out. "It has been my worst fear ever since I birthed you."

Aubrey's head snaps backward, taken aback by her mother's reply. She looks down at herself, trying to figure out what she meant. "See me like what?" Aubrey asks, baffled.

Nia turns her tearful gaze back toward her daughter, giving her vulnerability and honesty. "As a little girl, you were always so smiley and joyful. My favorite thing to do was watch you skip around, dance, and rollerblade. You lived in your own world of happiness, and my one goal was to help you hold on to that world forever. That's why I closed the door on you. You couldn't continue living in your perfect world of happiness and live here."

Aubrey looks over the outside of her suburban childhood home, pondering how something so beautiful can have so much darkness dwelling inside. She wonders if it is why her mother worked so hard to keep up the outside of the home—to mask its real identity.

"Looking at you like this feels like I'm looking at a corpse," Nia continues, tears falling rapidly. "Where is my joyful baby? Why aren't you laughing loudly and skipping around? I would do anything to see my girl with the big spirit rollerblade up this driveway again." Nia watches Aubrey's head fall in shame.

"I haven't seen that girl since I left her five years ago. That's why I'm back. I need to figure out how I can restore her."

Chapter Seventeen

UNABLE TO BRING HIMSELF to leave Ohio permanently without Aubrey, Daniel reports to Florida for training with just a small bag of workout clothes. He doesn't pack up his apartment. He doesn't say goodbye to his friends. He simply gets on a plane with his family by his side, intending to return to Ohio when time permits. Daniel, Delmain, Sylvia, and Kennedy settle into a luxury rental home on the beach. Daniel is standing in a bedroom looking out of a large picture window at waves crashing against the shore when he receives a call from Grant Lennox, confirming that he officially got an invite to the NFL Scouting Combine. Finally, he achieves the goal he worked diligently to accomplish over the past six months. With tears of joy, he opens his cell phone, typing in the first person he wants to share his good news with. When his search produces zero results, he remembers that he had deleted and blocked her number. Tossing his phone on the bed, Daniel falls face-first into a stack of plush pillows taking up the top of the bed. As he lies with his face in the fabric, he recalls how Aubrey's encouragement, wisdom, and patience reignited his belief that his goal was attainable. Daniel reaches out for his phone. He restores her number and her access to him. Opening their messages, he reads through the thread, reliving the love they once shared. She had gotten into the habit of sending him a morning message daily. The messages varied from inspirational, funny, or loving. No matter the message type, he looked forward to sharing her thoughts. When rereading their texts becomes too overwhelming, Daniel tosses the phone aside and reburies his head in the pillows.

He spends the following weeks rehabbing his hamstring and exercising with industry professionals to prepare for the combine. Every time he completes a training day, he feels like he is walking in his purpose. The only thing missing from his life is Aubrey. He finds himself wishing that Aubrey was there to join in on their family conversations and experiences. When Sylvia and Kennedy walk in from a day of shopping, it feels like Aubrey should be with them. When they gather to eat dinner, Daniel can't help but feel like a staple member of his family is missing. The more the days pass, the more consumed he becomes with missing her.

AFTER EIGHT WEEKS TRAINING, Daniel walks into Lucas Oil Stadium in Indianapolis, Indiana, where he will go through a series of tests to see if he is NFL material. He doesn't feel anxious or unprepared. On the contrary, he feels ready to dominate every test and show the coaches and team owners why they should want him. As he walks over the NFL logo painted on the ground, his intuition tells him it is the first time of many. He glances around the enormous stadium, suited for sixty-seven thousand fans. Most seats are empty because only a select few have an invitation. Daniel had imagined himself inside the stadium many times. He had looked up pictures online and cemented them into his memory. Now that it is his reality, he feels relaxed walking through the stadium as if he had done it a thousand times already.

The same relaxed feeling follows him when it comes time to perform. He walks out on the field confidently, ready to accomplish the dreams he has been mentally and physically preparing for. His first test is a catching drill. Digging his cleats into the turf, he takes off down the field. When he reaches the thirty-yard mark, he checks for the ball in the air. The ball is coming in hotter than he expects, seemingly heading out of bounds. Daniel picks up speed, jumps into the air, and catches the ball. While in midair, he realizes he is close to being outside the inbound line. Squandering the drill isn't an option for him. He maneuvers his body to release one foot to the turf and extends his second leg back so that both feet make it inside the line by the slightest margin. The odd landing throws off his balance, so to keep the football in his hand, he tucks his head into his chest and kicks up into an effortless front flip while maintaining possession of the ball. Onlookers clap, unable to contain their excitement by witnessing such an athletic move. Daniel delights in passing the test for only a half second before directing his thoughts back to dominating the remainder of the combine.

In his zone, he catches every ball and hits every mark. He jumps the highest vertical and bench presses the most weight out of his group. He has the best stats out of every wide receiver there. When the moment arrives for him to perform the all-important forty-yard dash, he feels nervous for the first time since he entered the stadium. It means everything to get a fast time. A slow forty-yard dash can negate his other accomplishments. Stepping up to the line, he breathes in and out audibly, knowing that if he breathes, his body can't hold on to the nervousness. He gets down in a three-point stance, feeling the turf between his fingers. He can hear Aubrey's voice reminding him to relax and run loose. He can hear her telling him to command his body. Listening to her voice, he relaxes and tells his body what to do. When it is time for him to begin, he takes off, driving his arms and lifting his knees as Aubrey had taught him. In a matter of seconds, he crosses the line. Looking over at the stop clock, Daniel sees the time 4.27 on the screen. It is the fastest time of the day and precisely what he needs to remind everyone of his athleticism and help them forget his faults. Most importantly, it is all he needs to secure his spot in the upcoming NFL draft. Daniel closes his eyes and rejoices within.

After dominating his performance, a reporter pulls Daniel aside to interview him. "Daniel Sane, the number one overall prospect. It's safe to say that this outcome is stunning, considering you didn't have a football season. Are you just as stunned?" the sports reporter asks, extending her microphone for his answer.

"I'm not stunned at all," Daniel replies confidently. "I made a plan and followed it, and everything worked out accordingly. Since I couldn't get out on the football field this season, I put in the work on the track, and here I am."

"What a perfect moment to let those watching know what you overcame and what it took to get here."

The reporter puts the microphone back in front of his mouth. Daniel simply smiles at how she tries to finesse information from him. "I had a bit of a rock bottom moment that altered my path, but I didn't let those things define me. I also didn't allow others to make me feel obligated to publicize my downfalls. We live in a world that teaches people to wear adversity like a badge of honor. Too many people are giving sickness and disorders glory. I want to glorify perseverance. I want to empower people to believe that nothing has the power to defeat them unless they give it that power. I'll never say what had me down, not because I'm embarrassed, but because the situation is dead; it doesn't deserve to have life. I won't speak dead words and give them energy in the atmosphere. So instead of normalizing defeat, limitation, lack, and failure, let's normalize rising up, cultivating your abilities, and walking in power."

The sports reporter pulls the microphone back to herself and looks into the camera with a surprised expression. "Wow," she breathes. "And there you have it. It's not much else to say after that."

Daniel bows his head, thanking the reporter for the interview, and walks off as the number one NFL draft prospect.

DANIEL REMOVES the last photo frame from the wall in his apartment, handing it to his mother to bubble wrap and place into the moving box. He moves about the apartment with a melancholy countenance, carelessly tossing everything into a box. He has been dreading the day he moved away from Ohio permanently. He feels like he's living a nightmare; Aubrey's presence can quickly shift it into a daydream.

Sylvia, Delmain, and Kennedy watch him with worried expressions. "Wake up on the wrong side of the bed?" Delmain confronts. "This is supposed to be one of the happiest times in your life. Why the long face?"

"What do you mean?" Daniel feigns confusion. "I'm just focused … getting my stuff done." His family knows him well enough to know that he isn't being honest, but they don't pressure him.

Daniel continues tossing things into the box. He pauses when he sees his Life Plan book. He opens the cover and sees Aubrey's handwriting on the pages. His emotional side considers tearing out the pages, crumpling them, and tossing them in the trash. The logical part of him prohibits him from doing so. A sentimental smile grows on his face as he stares at the paper. He remembers Aubrey's encouragement and support that helped him push forward. She was the perfect example of a helpmate. Closing his eyes, Daniel combats the heaviness on his chest that appeared every time he thought about leaving her. He felt it would somehow be more manageable if he didn't see or speak to her. But it is still the most agonizing decision he has ever made. There are moments when staying in Ohio and forgetting about the NFL cross his mind. He loves Aubrey more than football but knows staying won't make a difference. He turns the page in the book and rereads the sentence she had written months before. Reconnect with my mom. It is a reminder that she simply isn't ready for him. It takes his breath away.

"Are you going to say goodbye to her?" His mother speaks in a tender voice.

He is standing like a statue in a daze. Snapping out of it, he puts the book in the box and shakes his head back and forth. "Doesn't matter anymore."

"Why not?" Kennedy asks.

Daniel looks around at his family. Each of their faces holds the same expression of disbelief. "Oh, so now you guys like her?"

"I never disliked her," Sylvia defends. "I didn't think you were settled enough to have a serious girlfriend while focusing on your goals. However, after hearing your speech on draft day, I realize how much you've grown. You have become a man. I apologize for treating you like a child."

"I apologize too, son," Delmain agrees. "If you feel like you love her, I respect your decision to be with her."

Daniel shrugs aggressively. "It doesn't matter at this point anyway." Daniel put one last book into the box. "That's everything. Let's get this stuff shipped off so we can go."

"What about this?" Kennedy holds up his track uniform.

Daniel turns over his wrist to look at his watch. "I'm supposed to meet Coach in a half hour to return that."

Chapter Eighteen

DANIEL WALKS INTO the empty arena with the uniform in his hand. The moment he steps on the track, his heart begins to race. He hadn't been back to the arena since he proposed to Aubrey. He can still feel the love thick in the air. It feels overpowering to be in the place where he and Aubrey spent the most time together. Trying to block out all the memories, he desperately glances around for Coach. He wants to return his uniform and beeline out of there. The place holds too many sweet memories and bitter reminders that Daniel can't be with his soulmate, no matter how magnetic their connection is. His bond with her feels more secure than his sister, dad, and even his mom. There isn't a doubt in his thoughts that she isn't the person he is supposed to become one with and create a future with. Instead, he has to begin his future without her and hope their time will come around again. It makes him physically ill.

Coach walks through a side door, his arms extended wide. "Congratulations!" he greets with a proud smile. "You did it!"

"Appreciate it, Coach," Daniel replies while falling into his hug to regain strength. "I can't thank you enough for taking a chance on me."

"I would do it again a thousand times over," Coach tells him.

Daniel nods in response, sensing Coach's sincerity. "You're the best, Coach." Daniel hands Coach the uniform, eager to end the conversation to get out of there.

Coach takes the uniform and stuffs it under his arm. "Before you go, I have a few people who want to say goodbye to you."

When Coach finishes his sentence, his track teammates start popping out of random places in the arena. "Surprise!" they yell. Some people are holding balloons. Two teammates start hanging a banner that says congratulations across the bleachers. Travis and Lily are walking toward him with a cake. Daniel's petulance doesn't leave much room for excitement. He loves their thoughtfulness, but he also feels ambushed. He isn't sure he is strong enough to face the beautiful heartache he has been eluding. Looking around at all his former teammates, he searches for one face. It isn't long before he finds her. The face stands out from the crowd—lively brown eyes that look just as apprehensive as he feels. Thick natural hair that frames her face perfectly. Plump, glossy lips. Milky brown skin blends over her body immaculately. He has successfully evaded her for months to avoid the very feeling breaking him at the knees as he gazes into her eyes. Being within feet of her makes the stutter in his heart even out. Her presence produces serenity, as if she is the answer to all his worries. It makes him angry. He wants to run out of the arena until he is far away from her. Daniel drops his eyes, unable to look at her for another second.

"You know we couldn't let you leave without celebrating you, bro," Travis says, clapping him on the shoulder.

"I should have known this was your idea," Daniel replies, his voice low and tense.

"Congratulations!" Lily sings, holding out the cake.

Daniel wraps his arm around Lily, hugging her. "Thanks, Lily!"

Daniel's teammates form a long line in front of him, taking turns congratulating him with big hugs and words of encouragement. After twenty minutes, the line dwindles to just a couple of people. Aubrey is one of them, standing at the end, chewing on the corner of her lip and fidgeting. Daniel imagines himself being close enough to smell and feel her soft skin beneath his hands. His imagination turns into kissing her while her little fingers wrapped in his diamonds rub up his chest. He shakes off the imagination as Aubrey steps in front of him.

"Congratulations, Daniel," she says in an even, soft tone. "You did it. You did everything you wrote in your plan." The words come out practiced. A subtle breath of relief escapes as if she accomplished a colossal feat.

"I did. Almost. I mean … I appreciate you. Thank you." The words stumble from his lips. He isn't as prepared as Aubrey. He runs a hand over his face, making his discomfort apparent.

"I got a notification that you're sharing your location with me again," Aubrey says lightheartedly. "I thought maybe it was an open invitation for me to visit you."

"I unblocked you, so that's what that was about," he replies, dismissing her bait. He doesn't want to be her vacation getaway. He wants to be her home.

Not knowing how else to reply, Aubrey nods.

Daniel doesn't know what to say to her either. They awkwardly stare at each other. They see so many unanswered questions, hurt, and a depth of love in each other's gaze. The combination of emotions is intolerable to Daniel. He has held in too much for too long. He turns to Travis, begging him to come to his rescue with a look. Travis jogs over to stand between them, giving Daniel a chance to pivot quickly and walk away without a proper farewell.

"Daniel has to get going, so we're going to cut the cake," Travis announces to cover the tense moment.

Aubrey mashes her lips together to stop them from quivering. Tears slowly fill her eyes, exposing her as everyone watches their interaction. Their teammates had been curiously anticipating what the Daniel and Aubrey reunion would look like. They had heard about how she rejected his proposal, and they tuned in to witness the retaliation.

"Thanks, everyone, for the love. I appreciate each one of you. Unfortunately, I have to catch a flight tonight, so I must get going. I love y'all," Daniel states to his teammates, his eyes avoiding Aubrey.

As he walks out of the arena, a gravitational pull hinders him from jumping in his car and driving away. He stops walking and turns back toward the arena entrance. Aubrey is standing ten feet behind him, profusely wiping her eyes, trying to pull herself together before approaching him. Daniel huffs out a tired sigh, hating to see her cry, hating the strain between them. He walks to where she is standing.

Aubrey pats her face dry, demanding the tears to stop flowing. "Ugh," she grumbles, mad at herself for losing control. "All I wanted was to say bye to you."

Daniel doesn't respond. He just looks at her blankly. He doesn't want to say goodbye.

"Please stop being mad at me," she requests.

He releases another sigh. "I'm not mad at you. I'm mad your bags aren't packed, and my ring isn't on your finger."

"It'll happen," Aubrey assures him.

"In a few years, right?" Daniel recites her words bitterly.

Aubrey keeps her mouth closed to avoid the same dance that leads them nowhere. Aubrey can't say what the future holds for her and her mom. She just knows she wants to explore it.

"You can't see your future because you're stuck in your past. You know that, right?" Daniel delivers the words he feels she needs to hear.

"Just like you need your mom, I need mine," Aubrey says, trying to get him to empathize.

Dropping his gaze to the ground, Daniel simply nods. He knows that Aubrey needs to stay and figure out her life, and he needs to man up and let her go. "I got a flight to catch."

"Are we going to keep in touch?" Aubrey asks in a pleading tone.

"Sure, we'll keep in touch," he tells her. Bending down, Daniel gently touches his lips to the top of her head. His lips are tight like he doesn't want to relinquish the fullness of his love to her.

Aubrey usually feels a warm tingle rush through her whenever he kisses her, but this kiss gives her a chill. "Why does it feel like you're letting me go?"

"You remember that piece of your heart I wanted so badly?"

Aubrey nods.

"I need to give it back. It didn't belong to me in the first place."

"What do you mean?" Aubrey asks, her eyes blinking as fast as her heart is beating. "Are you saying you want this to be the end of things?"

Daniel shakes his head. "I'm saying that you were right. Your heart belongs to the one who formed you in your mother's womb." He smiles as he repeats her words. "Mine does too. So, let's lead our hearts that way, and when it's time for us to come back together, it'll happen. I look forward to it." A broken yet loving smile creeps over his mouth. Aubrey smiles back just as lovingly. She wraps her arms around his neck, squeezing him tightly. Daniel would have been content to stay there all night with her, but it simply isn't where he's supposed to be anymore. "I'll call you when I get there."

WHEN DANIEL ARRIVES in Houston, he does not let Aubrey know. He is acclimating to a new city and meeting with NFL teams, coaches, and potential teammates. His phone constantly rings. Almost every call is Aubrey. "Hey, Bree," he answers, his tone emotionless.

"Hey." She pauses, surprised that he answered the phone. "You must be super busy. I haven't heard from you since you left. It's been a week."

"I do have a lot going on. What's up, though? Did you need something?"

Aubrey sits quietly for a beat, wondering why he seems withdrawn. "No, I don't need anything. I wanted to hear your voice and about how everything is going."

"Everything's great. Texas feels like home," he says, giving her the abridged version.

"Okay," she replies in a short tone. Daniel's standoffish behavior annoys her.

"I got a meeting I need to get to. I'll text you tomorrow."

"You'll text me tomorrow..." She repeats his words, wanting him to hear how he comes across.

"Yeah, I'll text you tomorrow."

"Is that how you want to communicate from now on?"

"Yeah."

"Wow. Okay." His words sting, but she isn't going to beg him to talk to her.

"I love you, Bree Bree."

His sincere sentiment confuses and annoys Aubrey even more. "You love me," she echoes inconsolably.

"Yep, I really do. I'll text you tomorrow." Without another word, he ends the call. Part of letting Aubrey grow means he must no longer be available to her like he used to be.

Giving him space, Aubrey occupies her time by catching up with her mom. They spend hours on the phone chatting. On the weekends, Aubrey drives across the state line to spend a few hours with her in the flower bed. When Aubrey is in her mom's presence, she lays her head on her shoulder, feeling her nurturing touch. Rekindling the relationship brings Aubrey so much happiness that she doesn't have time to miss Daniel.

For two months, she eagerly drives up and down the highway anticipating a hug and quality time with her mom. Finally, accustomed to their established mother-daughter routine, Aubrey pulls up to her mom's house and steps out of the car. She is wearing a beautiful cocktail dress.

"Oh, you look nice," Nia compliments. "Where are you coming from?"

"I thought it would be cool if we went to brunch. My treat. Go put on something cute and let's step out."

Nia pretends not to hear Aubrey's statement. Instead, she slides on her gardening gloves and bends to her knees.

"Did you hear me?"

"I'm not hungry."

"Okay," Aubrey says, picking up on her odd reaction. "Well, how about we walk around the neighborhood? It's such a beautiful morning."

"I don't want to leave this house," Nia clarifies.

"Why," Aubrey questions.

Nia removes her dirty gloves, dropping them on the ground as she stands to look Aubrey directly in the eyes. "Aubrey, I need you to hear me. I made my choice," she begins. Her hardy tone makes Aubrey square her shoulders. "I chose to stay in this house because I have unfinished business here, but you don't belong here."

"I need my mom," Aubrey states, interrupting whatever point Nia is about to make.

Nia grabs Aubrey's face.

"No, Aubrey. No, you don't. Baby, look at your capacity to love. I didn't call. I didn't show up for you, yet you're standing here. Even when you feel empty, love flows from you."

Tears sting Aubrey's eyes, threatening an emotional outpouring. Aubrey shakes her head to deny her mom's words and the tears that threaten to invade her calm.

Nia rushes to continue her statement before Aubrey can jump in. "I apologize. I didn't give you my best. But don't you know who you are? You are powerful. You can't be broken."

"Mom," Aubrey cuts her off.

"You are worthy," Nia continues, determined. "You are valuable. You deserve way more love than I could ever give you here. You don't belong here."

"I need my mom," Aubrey cries out. "I need my mom."

Nia wraps Aubrey in her arms and hugs her tightly. Aubrey melts against her mom's body, only for Nia to push her away.

"Whatever you're looking for, Aubrey, it's not here. It never was."

Aubrey stands pensive, her eyes diverting back to the two-story home. The outside of the house is beautiful. It is the kind of place you drive by and desire to live in, not knowing what's inside. Aubrey lived there her whole life and didn't know.

"Aubrey ... Baby. Don't come back here," Nia says, resolute.

Aubrey looks away from the house and back to her mom, wondering what was so bad that it made her incapable of being a parent. Whatever it is, Nia has convinced herself that Aubrey has no place there.

Corine Marie

Aubrey nods slowly as understanding sets in; this is a battle she isn't meant to win. She turns to get back in her car, closing the door behind her. Aubrey clicks her seatbelt into place and starts the engine. Nia comes to Aubrey's window, desperation in her eyes.

"I love you, Mom," Aubrey breathes sincerely.

Chapter Nineteen

DON'T COME BACK HERE. Aubrey replays Nia's words as she pulls onto campus. How can a mother deny her daughter affection ... recognition ... love when she urgently needs it, Aubrey thinks. "I love you, Aubrey," she says aloud to herself. Then, with resolve deep in her eyes, Aubrey elects herself as the person who will generously give the love she deserves. No more waiting and searching. "I'm going to love you even if no one else will." Aubrey reaches into the back seat to grab the rollerblades Daniel had gifted her months before. The white rollerblades with black straps and colorful wheels had tempted Aubrey many times over the past months. She didn't spare the skates a second thought, fearful of how far back they would take her.

With the rollerblades in hand, she enters the large wrought iron gate that leads to Growth Gardens. Under the late summer heat, every plant in the garden is prospering. Aubrey can see her sunflower the moment she walks through the gate, bright and tall against the summer landscape. Kicking off her shoes and stuffing her feet into the rollerblades, she prepares to skate over to admire the sunflower. Aubrey stands to her feet, finding her balance. Muscle memory takes over as she puts one foot before the other. The sound of wheels rolling over concrete transports her back to sixteen.

Aubrey was a young sixteen. Boys weren't the highlight of her focus. She wasn't sassing her mom. In fact, she relished her mom's approval. Aubrey remembers her mom pausing from the weeds in the flower bed to admire her rollerblading up the suburban street. She smiled so warmly at Aubrey that she felt it touch her. Lifting her hand to her mouth, Aubrey puckered up a kiss, blowing it in Nia's direction.

Her mom continued watching Aubrey as the wind twisted through her natural hair. Aubrey's arms and shoulders bounced in sync with the vibrations coming from her Air Pods. Her eyes were as bright as the setting sun kissing her skin. Aubrey danced and pranced on her rollerblades, savoring her mom's attentiveness. Aubrey frowned when her mom looked away to address her boyfriend standing behind the screen door. They exchanged a few words. When her mom turned back to Aubrey, a weariness was apparent in her eyes.

"Hey, Mom!" Aubrey sang, rolling up the driveway.

Pulling off her gardening gloves, she grabbed the front rail and pulled herself to her feet. She opened her arms, and Aubrey rolled directly into her embrace. She wrapped Aubrey tightly, holding onto her as if she was a little child. Aubrey was just as big as her mom, but she never shied away from one of her hugs. In fact, Aubrey craved them. Whenever her mom hugged her,

Aubrey experienced love saturating her entirely. It was as if the love leaked out and seeped into Aubrey. The feeling was overwhelmingly peaceful. Aubrey pressed her cheek against her mom's cheek, allowing the warmth to permeate. After a full minute of embracing, Nia pulled away to fix Aubrey's wind-blown curls. She maintained the pleasant smile, but Aubrey sensed her gloom. "Are you okay?" Aubrey asked.

"Of course I am," Nia lied smoothly. "I have a beautiful, happy daughter. You are happy, aren't you?"

Aubrey's brows pulled together as she studied her mom, trying to interpret what she genuinely meant to ask. Then, before she could figure it out, Nia's boyfriend returned to the door. "You cooking today?"

"I'm coming," Nia huffed before returning her attention to Aubrey. "I have to run in here." She moved quickly toward the front door. But, before going inside, she stopped to look over her shoulder. "Answer my question."

"Yeah, Mom. I'm happy," Aubrey answered sincerely.

She let out a relieved exhale and rushed into the house.

Aubrey sat down on the front stoop and removed her rollerblades. She sat still, allowing her bare feet to breathe. She wiggled her toes in the breeze while resting in the sun. Minutes later, she stood up to make her way inside the beautiful home, but when she turned around, her mother stood in the door frame. Nia wore a pained expression.

"Mom?" Aubrey questioned, her voice full of concern.

"Go to Lily's house," her mom instructed severely.

With wide eyes, Aubrey hesitated to follow her

instructions. "What happened?"

Nia slowly closed the front door and locked it. Aubrey turned away from the house, her bare feet pounding the pavement as she sprinted into the night. Aubrey's youth was over then. In a matter of minutes, the carefree young woman rebirthed into a worrisome adult.

Now twenty-one, rollerblading through Growth Gardens, Aubrey acknowledges her younger self. She admits feeling scared, lonely, and devalued when her mom pushed her out. Tears rush from her eyes, and Aubrey does not attempt to stop them. Instead, she embraces herself, consoling the younger, more innocent version of herself. "You're okay," she says to sixteen-year-old Aubrey. "You will soon realize that you are quite powerful."

Aubrey stops rollerblading when she reaches the sunflower. She stares up at its strong fifteen feet structure, admiring its radiance. Witnessing the difference from sprout to maturity reminds her of Adam's lesson about potential. The sunflower would've grown if it remained in its seedling pot. It could have been a pretty houseplant in someone's window. It would have survived, but without being grounded in rich soil with enough room to grow and generous daily sunlight, the sunflower wouldn't have become as vast with enough seeds to reproduce itself a thousand times. "If you would have stayed in that home, you were destined to settle for the mediocre version of yourself," Aubrey says, the lesson resonating. "Mom didn't abandon us. Instead, she gave us wings. That's the perception we will have moving forward." A final tear rolls down sixteen-year-old Aubrey's cheek, simultaneous with twenty-one-year-old Aubrey's smile.

THE NEXT MORNING, Aubrey lies in front of her window in the sunshine, writing in her journal. The alarm on her phone is buzzing, reminding her of her to-do list for the day. But the sun's warmth and comfort just won't release her. She feels swaddled in peaceful love and can't bring herself to move. She stays in that spot, allowing revelations to come to her. She realizes that even though she is in her apartment alone, she can feel a physical embrace. The feeling is familiar. Whenever she used to cry, longing for a mother's presence, that embrace kept her from falling apart. Every birthday and holiday she spent alone, that embrace kept her company. Every time she needed motherly advice, that all-knowing embrace told her what to do. The nurturing she thought she needed to stay in Ohio to receive was with her the entire time. It is within her.

After properly reflecting on her past, Aubrey starts writing out what she wants for her future. First, she makes a list of all her desires. Next, she writes out the top things she envisions clearly. Finally, when she puts her pen down, she sees that the future she wants isn't in Ohio anymore.

It only takes Aubrey ten minutes to pack up what she wants to keep. She gets rid of the few items left in her apartment and buys a one-way ticket to Houston. She boards the first available flight and is off to pursue new endeavors. Finally, she is ready to pursue her future.

Aubrey doesn't inform Daniel that she is coming.

Since he is still sharing his location with her, she opts to surprise him. After getting off the plane, Aubrey opens her phone, searches Daniel's location, and takes an Uber to the smoothie bar where he is. Toting just a small leather bag, Aubrey walks into the smoothie bar. She spots Daniel immediately. He is sitting at a small table with a guy and two women. The guys sit next to each other, and the women sit across from them. The woman across from Daniel talks animatedly while Daniel leans back in his chair, sipping on a green smoothie and listening intently. He laughs at whatever she says, his chin lifting and his eyes closing. When he reopens his eyes, he sees Aubrey standing by the entrance with her bag. His laughter comes to a halt. He stares, unmoving. Aubrey stands frozen, too, everything around her seeming to blur while Daniel remains in focus. They gaze at one another, Daniel wondering if his eyes are deceiving him while Aubrey tries to figure out what is different about him. Putting his smoothie on the table, Daniel slowly stands and approaches Aubrey. The moment they are close enough to touch, Daniel and Aubrey simultaneously wrap each other in their arms. Daniel lifts her from the ground. Making good use of her dangling legs, Aubrey wraps them around Daniel, securing herself to his body. They hold on to each other, breathing in each other's scents. Finding a home in each other's warmth. They hold to each other for so long that it becomes uncomfortable for onlookers. Neither Aubrey nor Daniel pays attention to the awkward gazes coming their way. Aubrey only gives attention to the way his muscles feel around her body. Football training has bulked him up, and she can't deny that she likes it. She wraps him even tighter in her arms. Daniel releases his hold when he feels excited about how she is clinging to him. Aubrey reluctantly lets him go, standing back on her feet.

"You're here," he says, his tone full of disbelief.

"I'm here," Aubrey repeats.

Daniel looks over his shoulder at the people he was sitting with, then back to Aubrey. Looking around him, Aubrey notices the girl he was sitting across from, giving her a strange once-over.

"Why didn't you tell me you were coming?" Daniel asks.

Aubrey simply shrugs, unable to articulate the urge she felt to get out of Ohio.

Daniel scratches his head while nodding. He doesn't seem pleased with the surprise. He looks back at the table once again. Aubrey's excitement starts to fade as she notices his reserved behavior. Thinking back over the past months, she remembers that they haven't truly communicated, even though they kept in touch daily through text. All their conversations were friendly—they texted about everything except their relationship status. Aubrey looks around Daniel again to look at the woman he had been sitting with. She is stunning. Jet black silk hair falls at her backside. Her skintight dress and stilettos make her stand out from all the casually dressed people in the smoothie bar, but she is confident, nonetheless. She seems to be the type of woman that can easily land a modeling contract or be the face of any makeup brand. She looks like a life-sized melanin barbie.

"You have a girlfriend," Aubrey says, the words matter-of-factly.

"I have a fiancée," Daniel corrects softly.

A painful ache starts in Aubrey's stomach and

begins rising to her heart. Everything around her turns hazy, so she closes her eyes. She can feel the vein in her head pulsing. She can hear a ringing in her ears. A scream threatens to explode from within. Aubrey covers her mouth to subdue her voice. As much as she wants to be mad, she can't be. It is her fault. She had given him unrealistic parameters.

"I asked this woman to marry me, and she said, yes, in a few years," Daniel reminds her.

Unable to speak, Aubrey nods.

"I'm just waiting for those years to pass," he continues.

Confused, Aubrey opens her eyes, searching back and forth between his eyes. "Are you talking about her or me?"

"I've only ever asked one woman to marry me," he clarifies as he simpers.

"Don't play with me like that."

Daniel chuckles, finding himself funny.

"So why do you seem nervous?" she questions.

"I'm not nervous."

"You're acting weird," she accuses.

"I'm trying to figure out how to act. Are you here for a weekend visit? You only brought one bag?" Daniel asks safe questions to avoid ambushing her with all his heart's desires.

"I never had that much stuff, to begin with."

"So, you're here to stay?"

"Here to stay," Aubrey confirms.

A million thoughts travel through his mind, and he thinks of a million questions he wants to ask. Does Aubrey plan on having her own space or moving in with him? If she wants to move in with him, does that mean she is ready to get married? Before he has a chance to ask, his friends approach. The guy is looking at Daniel with a playful expression. He puts his arm around Daniel and sets his sights on Aubrey. Checking her out, he admires her athleisure outfit—a one-shoulder sports bra, matching leggings, an oversized zip-up hoodie that's open and showing off her Olympic-ready shape, and sunglasses on top of her head.

"If I had to guess, I'd say you're Aubrey. Daniel mentions you like a hundred times a day."

Daniel laughs, not denying it. "This is my potential teammate, Kingston," Daniel introduces.

"You keep saying potential. Everybody knows you're going to be a Texan." Kingston turns his dialogue toward Aubrey. "Until he gets that official jersey, I guess I'm just potential."

Aubrey giggles. She reaches out her hand to shake his, but Kingston pulls her into a big hug.

"And this is his fiancée, Mila, and his little sister, Baylor." Daniel continues the introductions.

Aubrey notices how Daniel introduces Baylor as Kingston's little sister instead of just his sister. It is almost like he is intentionally separating himself from her. Baylor is the stunning woman who sat across from Daniel. When Aubrey first walked in, Baylor looked at her strangely. Aubrey observes the situation carefully. Though Baylor looks youthful, Aubrey doesn't find anything little sister-ish about Baylor. Instead, she is a gorgeous young woman with all her curves on display for Daniel to enjoy. Mila gives Aubrey a tight squeeze, warmly welcoming her. Baylor hugs Aubrey also, but her hug is less friendly, like she is just being polite. "And this beautiful woman is Aubrey," Daniel says, unsure how to introduce her. She had declined the title of his wife. Girlfriend isn't an accurate label, and he can't think of a word to describe how they are profoundly connected.

DANIEL DRIVES AUBREY to the home he has been staying in for the past couple of months. When they enter the house, Aubrey looks around the spacious home, taking note of the empty walls and unpacked boxes.

"Still haven't settled in?" Aubrey inquires.

"Kennedy offered to decorate, but I didn't want my sister's touch on my house this time. I wanted..." He doesn't finish the statement. "You want to see the rest of the house?" he asks, avoiding Aubrey's curious eyes.

She noticed that he was quiet during the drive to the house. His initial excitement to see her has faded. Instead, he is reserved, as if he is protecting himself from her. "Of course," she replies in a soft tone.

Daniel leads her into the kitchen. Aubrey drags her fingers over the marble countertops and marvels at the big window over the sink. The window gives her an impeccable view of the spacious backyard.

"Is that a pool?" she asks, squinting her eyes to get a better look.

Daniel flips a switch that lights up the backyard, so she can see the pool and hot tub. Aubrey opens the backdoor and kicks off her shoes to dip her toes in the water. It is perfectly warm.

"And there's a greenhouse back here!" She remembers him saying that he would move into a home with a greenhouse for her to retreat daily.

"Yep," he says with insistent dryness.

They move on to the home gym, offices, and plethora of bedrooms until they end in the master bedroom. It is the only room in the house with furniture and appears lived in. Daniel sits in a corner chair and slumps as if she drained all his energy.

"What's wrong?" she asks.

"What do you think of the house?" he asks instead of answering her question.

"It's a beautiful house. Empty though. Can't believe you've been living like this for months."

"Haven't had much free time. Football requires a lot from me."

Aubrey nods. "I've noticed. I haven't had much access to you either."

Daniel doesn't react to her comment. Instead, he merely gazes at her, his face expressionless. "That's not why you haven't been able to access me."

Aubrey nods again. "I've lost my access privileges," she states, understanding precisely what he is saying. Aubrey watches as Daniel sits in his chair, arms folded and his demeanor strictly business. It makes the environment feel sterile.

"What are your plans, Aubrey?" he interrogates impatiently. "You said you're here to stay. So where are you staying?"

"I booked a room downtown. I have a few months of savings. I plan to get a job and figure things out from there."

"Okay," he replies.

Aubrey waits for him to say something else, but he doesn't. He continues sitting in his chair with the same empty expression. "Okay," Aubrey huffs, frustrated because she isn't getting anything from him. "I'll call for a car and get out of your way," she says, testing him.

"Okay," he utters in the same empty tone, failing her test.

She pulls her phone from her bag and opens the ride app. The earliest car would get to her in twenty minutes. As she thinks of scheduling the pickup and bolting away from his coldness, she realizes she is doing something she told herself she wouldn't do anymore. Aubrey flew to Texas to do things differently than she did in the past. No more running. No more avoiding vulnerability. No more indecisiveness. She is there to reunite with Daniel, but instead of reuniting with him, she is putting more space between them. "My plans are to be with you," she states transparently. "That's why I came here. That is my plan."

Daniel raises his brows, finally giving her some kind of reaction. "And what does being with me look like for you?"

A small smile spreads on Aubrey's face as she realizes what he is doing. "I get it. You want to know what intentions I have for you."

He points to her, letting her know that she is correct. "I've always been the one professing my feelings and pursuing you. I've always wanted you as a full-time gig, but you were part-timing me. I haven't changed, but hopefully, you have because I won't deal with any more back and forth. I need love too." He speaks blatantly, withholding the bravado. Her rejection has deflated his trust, and he wants to clarify it.

Aubrey reaches into her bag and pulls out her journal. She opens it up to a page with MY FUTURE LIFE written in bold letters across the top. She hands

---

the journal to Daniel.

As his eyes scan the page, the corners of his lips begin to lift into a smile. "I want to start a business for people to meditate, rest, and renew. Maybe a spa or retreat home," he reads from the page while nodding in approval. "I want to marry Daniel and have his little Daniel babies." The smile turns into a massive grin. "One boy and one girl. We can name the boy Daniel, but the girl cannot be named Danielle. That's too corny." The grin turns to full-blown laughter.

"I finally rewrote my past and now I'm ready to create my future. And every time I imagine my future, I see you. This is my future. I get to choose if I'll live life sheltering myself from potential predators or escape that prison and unveil this love I have inside. I've never bonded with anyone so quickly and deeply as I did with you. Don't tell Lily, but you're the dearest friend I've ever had. I want that back. I want us."

"You're allowing me in?" Daniel asks.

"You can come in."

"I get to know you like that?"

His words tickle her. She lights up with a giggle. "Yep, I'm ready to know you like that."

"And we're going to take this commitment seriously, right? You can't get mad about something small and try to leave me."

"We're bonded spiritually, so as long as our spirits are moving toward the same purpose, that's how long you'll have me."

"I'm here for it."

"So, what's next?" Aubrey wonders aloud.

"Let's keep building ourselves as individuals, and when the time is right, we'll get married," he tells Aubrey. "In the meantime..." He stands from his chair and walks over to the bed. He opens the top nightstand drawer, removes a small box, and lifts the lid revealing the ring he had presented to Aubrey once before. "No rush. I'll wait a few years for you."

Aubrey extends her left hand for him to slide the halo of diamonds over her finger.

Note From the Author

It was not a good idea for me to date during my formative years. Obtaining love from a boy felt too critical. Separating from my mom and dad and entering foster care at a young age left me desperate for connection. I wanted a person in this world. I was looking for someone who understood me and made me feel stable. I put too much pressure on my mates to love me in a way that parents loved their children. I had a void too big for any boy to fill. My mental health needed intensive care.

I was that girl who entered relationships and relinquished the most precious parts of me in exchange for love. When those relationships ended with me receiving less than I desperately desired, I felt swindled out of my invaluable treasure. I had no one, and I had no self-respect. I became suicidal. Fortunately, my attempts weren't successful.

In my darkest moments, an intangible embrace provided my only consolation. Therefore, I began welcoming the intangible world. My mental health improved greatly when I opened my mind to the intangible, since the mind is nonphysical. I began giving intensive care to those unseen parts of me–my self-esteem, self-respect, self-worth, and self-love.

Everything I desired from someone else, I learned how to give it to myself. It was through loving myself that I was able to eliminate the sense of desperation and fill the void in my life, allowing me to build healthier relationships.

When writing this book, I reimagined the younger version of myself on her journey to self-love. The character Aubrey is in many ways a representation of me giving advice to my younger self. I didn't want Aubrey to experience the same traumas as me. I needed her to navigate her world in a way that she would overcome unscathed. That is my hope for every person reading this book. May you value yourself in a way that leads an abundant life. May you be rich because you know your worth. May you romanticize self-love more than loving anyone else.

Acknowledgments

First and foremost, I would like to express my deepest gratitude to God for His abundant blessings and unwavering guidance throughout this incredible journey. God's presence in my life has been the driving force behind my creativity and the source of my inspiration.

To my family, thank you for your endless love, unwavering support, and understanding during the creation of this book. Your encouragement and your belief in me have been like air to me. I am truly grateful for you.

I want to extend a heartfelt thank you to my beta readers. Your enthusiasm, constructive criticism, and valuable insights have played a vital role in shaping this book. Your input has enhanced the story's depth and ensured its quality, and for that, I am sincerely grateful.

Lastly, all those who supported me along this journey. I am deeply grateful for each and every person who has played a part in its creation. Your belief in me and the unwavering support you have shown me along the way have made this dream a reality. My eyes have been opened and my heart has grown. I never imagined that

I would receive such love but it has been poured all over me from start to finish. Thank you!

With immense gratitude,

Corine Marie

About the Author

In her process of writing, Corine discovered that personal imagination can be a practice of internal healing. A quiet girl with loud thoughts, young Corine had a lot of friends she liked to laugh with. They did most of the talking, she listened and observed. All throughout this time, she kept a journal—writing poems, thoughts, and elaborate stories.

Corine strongly derives her work from her own experiences. Corine finds common ground between her personal life and the lives of her characters. For Corine, writing allows her to invoke memories and observations into the development of her characters.

Over time, Corine understood the process of using fiction to rewrite her past life experiences. You can subtly address past mistakes with newfound wisdom. You can "reimagine the self."

Corine writes with her daughter in mind—a picture of her younger self. She considers her own life lessons and those of others who impacted her, then asks: How could this have been better? What is the lesson here? These lessons inform the re-imagined landscape of her stories, in which the characters represent alternative ways of knowing and being.

Biography written by Angel Evans

Made in the USA
Monee, IL
13 July 2023

38584435R00125